GRAM MOTHER

by

Jaqi Loye-Brown

MT-Ink.co.uk

First published by MT Ink in 2019

© Jaqi Loye-Brown

ISBN: 978-1-9164784-3-5

Cover design: MT Ink

Jaqi Loye-Brown asserts the moral right to be
identified as the author of this work

You give me just a taste, so I want more
Now my hands are bleeding and my knees are raw
'Cause now you've got me crawlin', crawlin' on the floor
And I've never known a girl like you before

- Edwyn Collins

Jaqi Loye-Brown

Contents

Jaqi Loye-Brown

Hoodie-winked

"Archie. Archie. Arrrchieeee!"

Incoherent teen vocals emanating from the bedroom and the hollow foot tapping accompaniment were standard background noise in the ground floor maisonette. A source of great irritation for Archie's mother since her son hit puberty.

She was disgruntled by his passion for music. Not content with listening to these relentless beats, despite her best efforts to the contrary, he was now producing tracks for his friends and building his channels on YouTube and Instagram.

Her hopes for him were dashed after he expressed a keen interest in technology. She was under the impression that he would take a scientific route. To this end she had inadvertently funded what she thought was equipment to progress in this field, buying endless apps and tech gear, as requested.

Archie had successfully picked up on his mother's weakness and exploited her ignorance. As a result, his bedroom was kitted out for his 'studies' with affordable 'DJ kit' on standby for world domination. Archie was a self-confident young person growing into his face, at ease with himself in spite of his mother's "peculiarities".

The limed oak door with enamel knob, twisted back and forth erratically. "Archie. Open the door...for fuck's sake. I'm going crazy, here!"

Archie reluctantly adjusted the position of his

headphones and cried out. "What? What now?"

"Open the frickin' door, matey. I'm not shouting through it anymore."

Size ten Vans stomped clumsily across the room, crashing through a barricade of stale coffee mugs and encrusted plates. The door finally opened, Archie huffing as he pushed past on his way out.

"Oi, where are you going?"

"Out..."

"Don't talk to me like that. Come back."

He stopped at the bottom of the stairs and turned to eyeball his mother. "I'm going out. Don't text. Don't wait up."

Art To Heart

With one firm hand at the wheel of his well worn 1991 diesel 2.15 T5 Landrover Defender Trotty pulled up to the Muswell Hill kerbside. After a heavy creaky pull on the handbrake, he turned to Myrtle. "Wait here darling. Back in two mins."

"It's fine, I know the drill, hun," chuckled Myrtle. As she unbuckled the seat belt, she was blinded by the sunset so settled back in the lived-in leather upholstery. She wondered for a brief moment whether her teenage daughter, Severign, was doing her homework. The end of school term was fast approaching. This was always such an expensive time. She cast her mind back to how she met Trotty, seven or so years ago, on a watercolour short course in Chelsea she had enrolled on to boost her fine art degree. How they connected in the refectory over a bad coffee. How they howled over their introduction.

"Sorry, I'm Guy Fox, but everyone calls me Trotty."

"As in, shall we?" gestured Myrtle, mimicking the foxtrot followed by a curtsey. "Or as in poo pants" as she mimed an arse wipe.

"Well, that's a first."

He was immediately ingratiated to her by her humour. They had become firm friends ever since. She from Winchester, a childhood spent with grandparents in Dorchester and he from Exeter. Both attended independent schools, had plummy accents and similar family values growing up.

She harked back to the first time she discovered why he was a bit of a 'face'. Well, a socialite-lite, at least. In the past their club scene paths had crossed unknowingly. Acid house fields and secret urban raves meant they shared a cultural understanding. He lived somewhere in Battersea, not that she had ever been invited inside, and seemed to have friends from a variety of creative backgrounds. He had fast-tracked her into his colourful social circle of thespians, PR pros, gallery owners, filmmakers and club promoters, not to mention one or two trustafarians. The duo swanned around town spuriously...launches, first night openings and intimate chichi soirées made all the more enjoyable because it involved indulging her two favourite passions, Rioja and coke, and not the Kalimotxco Spanish delectation either.

Their relationship was magical. He a tall, grey, dashing artisan, she a cool leggy, blonde. Both with a convivial, social arm. It was just as well. Trotty was a dealer, serving up on London's finest Boho to Soho scenes. He scurried about with his messy hair and steely blue eyes, in an assortment of vintage, crinkled blazers, looking every bit a comic caricature of a bumbling clumsy artist.

He had a steady hand in multidisciplinary art and had exhibited around the UK and Europe over the years. As Myrtle adjusted the Defender's well-worn sun visor her mind turned to the first time she saw his exquisite paintbox. The gold, trace of his grandfather's initials 'Master A A FOX Jnr' on the ebony wood, which he claimed was carved in India. It was a heavy, substantial bit of kit. Once opened, it revealed a host of tubes and tiny cans of paint, colour and oils. An array of art paraphernalia...brushes, spatulas, splattered rags, scattered on top of the paints.

Trotty always kept the box with him. Even mid-painting on the water colour course, she noted how it never left his side, he would carefully pack up and take the box with him to the refectory for a coffee break. A loveable idiosyncrasy she thought of the talented man. Quite normal for an artist to behave oddly.

He would paint adorable calling cards on small offcuts of canvas, which he also carried in a leather folder.

"The carvings on your box are immense."

"Oh darling, aren't they just," chirped Trotty. "You peeping Tom, you..."

"Hah. I didn't mean your box, I meant your ...erm...your box. Unless that's intricately sculpted as well?"

"Myrtle Sandwell, it is deodar cedar wood and was made for my grandfather as a child when my great grandfather worked at the Indian High Commission. Apparently, the sculptor was not dissimilar in age to my young grandfather at the time, around 10 years old. All local materials apparently...and there is magic in this box."

"Is it spooked? Do the carvings have some kind of hidden meaning?"

"Ahah...the forbidden is very much within," gestured the jester. "All is not what it seems..."

With over dramatic interplay of his fore fingers, the rest splayed out like wings, Trotty teased the box open. Beyond the paints visible, out slid two drawers filled with dozens and dozens of wraps of coke. A single gram measure in neat little folded parcels.

It was Myrtle's widened eyes and even more gasping mouth that tickled Trotty the most. She needed cheering up and it seemed like the right time.

"Ooof, Trots...you are full of surprises. Let's tuck

in," she chuckled.

"Oh Myrt...you're a classy one. Why not...hope it'll perk you up a little."

"Yes and yes. This refectory is pants, let's get wine."

All this happened around the time she moved in with boyfriend Marko. He had just procured a license for his second tiny bar between Queens Park and Kensal Green. The drink on tap caused tension between them within the first few weeks of opening. Romance had suddenly dissipated as their existence on wine and coffee took its toll. Myrtle would have left him had it not been for daughter, Severign, who was only 12 at the time. It was not fair to burden her with yet another upheaval.

They had witnessed a bad temperament Marko had conveniently kept hidden until they were trapped in his lair. Now Myrtle had given him the last of her savings towards his investment, she felt financially beholden to him.

She couldn't ask her parents for a penny more. She still owed 5k she borrowed from them to get out of another boyfriend shaped hole and credit card bill.

Wistfully, she recalled how wasted she and Trotty had got after racking up four lines from one gram in as many minutes. That was the week she left Severign with her father, Boyd, when the fighting with Marko had seared past boiling point.

"Myrt..."

Trotty tapped the windscreen as he failed to open the Land Rover. "Sorry, darling, I was away with the fairies - as usual...hah."

"I was a bit longer, but I think that's me done for the evening. A little earlier than expected. Shall we do something? Have you got to get back to that tosser?"

"Ugh, please, I've come here to escape that rotter, Trotters. Hey that rhymes. Should've been a rapper."

"Hmmm, I dunno. A wrapper of what? Haha."

"Tch, I'm hungry. Fancy a tapas?"

"A'huh. I know just the place."

"Could you cover me, Trotts, my love. Just until next week. I've actually sold a bloody painting, but it's taking weeks for the money to transfer. Painful. I should receive something soon."

"You've been stuck with that oik for too long...sorry, Myrt. He's been very bad for you and possibly worse for Sev. You've got to leave him."

They sat across from each other at the taverna, the reflection of the rustic candlelight on their Rioja filled glasses.

"I was just thinking back to the time you first showed me your art box, Trots. I should've left him back then. Time has just flown. Severign's turning sixteen soon and I can't afford to do anything for her. Her dad and my parents will cover it all as usual, but I feel like I've let her down. Anyway, I just can't seem to get going...ooh yum, these garlic prawns..."

"They are yum. Good call. But darling, if you stay, there's only going to be more of the same. Get another job..chalk painting and upcycling shabby chic tat isn't making you what you need to live on."

"I love it, though, darling. If I do some shifts in the shop Dande lets me use the workshop for free...and I get to keep all the money from sales of my own projects. My easel is there too, so I still paint. It's a great arrangement, plus she's such fun."

"Darling, darling, you don't have to explain yourself to me. I'm not Marko and certainly not Boyd. However, fun as Dande is, to all intents and purposes you are little more than her glorified intern."

"Steady. She's a good friend. Besides, it makes Severign happy because I'm saving the planet. Haha."

Severign was generally conscious about climate change, expressing similar values without invitation. She avoided wearing make-up because she was not convinced it was an ethical industry. She moisturised with cruelty free skin care and vegan make up ranges, without animals derivatives, no palm oil wherever possible choosing to stick to just one brand, PETA recognised. When she ran out she raided the larder for natural coconut oil.

"Shall I order another bottle?" asked Trotty, tipping the last drops into their glasses.

"Hmmm, yes please."

"How does Sev feel about tosspot? Does she know what's going on? Her dad even?"

"No, no, I think she hears the odd thing, but she's a bright girl. She knows what he's like. As long as he doesn't bother her."

"What?"

"Oh my God, Trotty, I would scratch his fucking eyeballs out if he tried anything. Don't even think it..."

Myrtle tried to calm herself down.

"Sorry, darling. I didn't mean anything. Let's change the subject. There's a perfectly good reason why I'm not in a relationship."

"Yes, you. Penelope was nice. As was Dominique and Georgina."

"I know. I'm a heartbreaker."

"What about Frank or Seanie, you leaning more towards the boys now?"

"Haha...maybe...how gorgeous was Sean?"

"I would, hah..."

"But he wouldn't of, hah..."

Myrtle gave a wry smile and laughed in her trademark posh chortle.

"Listen, Myrt...I need to tell you something, but you have to keep it to yourself."

"Okay, of course...what is it?"

"You know the Biennale in South Africa I've been banging on about?"

"The Joburg grant scheme thingy?"

"Yes...I'm in. I've been accepted on a year's residency. Isn't it incredible?"

"Come here, Trots, darling," Myrtle reached over the table. "Bloody well done you. You so deserve it. Mwaw."

"Thank you love. They called me yesterday. I'm just waiting for the written confirmation. But yes, I'm in. A lot of bloody pressure, though. Hope I'm up to it."

"Of course you are...where about is it... actually in Joburg?"

"Erm, no, you'll love this, a place called Cape Winelands."

"Surely not? That's a place? Hahaha, trust you. I'm so proud of you. I'm going to miss you...you've been the best thing to happen to me since Severign."

"Wow. This is getting just a little bit emoshe...and you're the only person I've told so far. Keep mum, Myrt."

"Count on it. But when do you leave?"

"That's what I'm waiting to hear. It's a different date from the closing date and the actual announcement. I have so much shit to sort out. I'm beginning to wonder if it will all be worth it."

"Careful what you wish for. Shall we celebrate properly?"

Myrtle raised her eyebrows and wriggled her

nose. Not the most sophisticated signal but Trotty knew what she meant and slipped her a wrap under the restaurant table.

After they had both separately availed themselves of the toilet facilities, the conversation resumed in earnest.

"I feel like we need to mark this auspicious occasion, Trots?"

"Hmmm, should we order some bubbles or head somewhere else?"

"Tell you what, why don't we head to your place. It's been at least five years or more and you've never so much as invited me in."

"And for good reason lady. C'mon, I'll get the bill."

Trotty hit the road in the Defender with noisy abandon. It was late and the roads were reasonably quiet. The route Myrtle thought he would take seemed to veer off towards North Kensington rather than Battersea.

"Have you got a late drop off to make?" asked Myrtle.

"Nope. We're heading to my other place. Just up here."

"What...here?" said a surprised Myrtle, peering at the white Regency style pillar-lined terrace in West-bourne Park.

"Yup. I did tell you that I'm caretaker of the flats here, didn't I?"

"Not sure. We've been here before, though. Didn't realise...you dark horse, you. Do you own it?"

"Yes and no. It's in the family trust with my brother...you know...the one in The City?"

"I thought your sister was in The City?"

"You're confused. My father's sister, my auntie, well, she's a name in The City."

"Well, I can't keep up. Are we going in?"

"Get out the car, silly girl."

Myrtle immediately recognised the tiled foot path and the wrought iron railings. The giant door and the hallway.

"Didn't we come here for a party in the basement and a BBQ on the roof terrace a couple of summers ago?"

"Can't believe you remembered either of those nights. You were properly trashed, cherubim."

"Never forget a big house. It…is…ginormous. And it's gorgeous. So one of these flats is yours?"

"Not quite. It's very complicated. I have to manage the property for a while first, so I get to stay here as a part of the deal."

"You lucky old fruit."

"It's not all good," whined Trotty, as he opened the door to the first floor flat.

"How so?"

"As the black sheep of the family, they sting me with these little traps so that I 'earn my keep' so to speak."

"I'm trapped by my family to the tune of five grand and that's bad enough. Know which I'd rather. But don't you live in Battersea?"

"Well, my darling… That. Is. A. Whole…other story. I've got some wine here somewhere…"

"It's a huge space. Mind if I look around?"

"No. Go ahead. There are three bedrooms, reception, a study and two bathrooms. Figure it out."

The home was modestly furnished with an eclectic mix of antique and modern styles. It had not been painted in some years, the mild tobacco stains a give-away. Seated on the floor of the giant pouffe in the centre of the high ceiling study, the pair continued the mutual 'love in' about how much they meant to each other.

They were friends. Good friends. Firm friends. No benefits ever mentioned or attempted, despite their partying ways.

Trotty treated 'Sev', as he called her, as if she was his own. Nurtured her artistic leanings and her increasing interest in her carbon footprint. He would send her useful links on social media and take her and her mother on 'painting away days' to explore nature, flora and fauna...trying different mediums. These trips used to melt Myrtle's heart. It hurt that Severign took no interest in art. Trotty switched the lamp lights on for her.

"I'm glad you finally invited me here. I feel like I really know you now."

"Well, I felt a bit guilty about it to be honest. In my line of work — said the gambler to the dealer — I have had to play my cards close to my chest."

"Speaking of which, isn't that a Jean-Baptiste..."

"...Siméon Chardin..., yes, well spotted! It's 18th Century, and pretty rare. Trust you, none of your Annie Sloan upcycled pieces in here."

"Don't knock it...You should try her chalk paint in your next project. It's addictive. It really is."

"Shall we?"

"Oh, alright, twist my arm, then."

"You were born twisted."

"Ah, you finally understand me..."

"Actually, Myrt, I do. I trust you implicitly. It's not something I think I've ever said. But I really trust you."

Nervously, Myrtle was''t sure where the conversation was heading and scoffed it off, as she usually did when faced with it.

"When I throw shade, I consider the light and dark of the hues involved," she bluffed, troubled by his confession of trust, because she knew he was wrong about her.

Since they met, Myrtle had been struggling to pay off her running tab with him for the gear he had supplied her. With the 'eight ball' she usually had on tick each week from Trotty (an eighth of an ounce or roughly three and a half grams) she was already selling to friends at either an inflated price, or with a small amount skimmed off each gram, and replaced with bicarbonate of soda. The surplus was then 'up-cycled' for personal use or to help create another sale.

What with school trips, laptops and rent, she could never make ends meet. She still had expensive taste beyond her means, a hangover from an excessive eighties lifestyle.

She was the one plagued with guilt because Trotty never harangued her for the debt. In fact, he was always so generous. The more he let her off the more she seemed to procure. He was a complete darling.

Bedlam

Myrtle pulled up in her Mini outside the school gates, careful to ensure that the engine was turned off, leaving the hazards on as a concession.

"Hi, Mum. Guess who came in to give us a talk today?"

"Who is that boy, I saw you with?"

"No one. Can I go and stay at Daddy's again please?"

"Don't change the subject. Who is he? He's older and not in uniform. Who is he, Severign?"

"I told you, no one. Will you drop me off?"

"No. You're doing your homework. No slacking off. I'm making vegetable carbonara with that vegan cheese you like. Don't think I'm letting this boy thing go."

"I've already done most of my homework. We have study periods for that now. I hate it at home."

"Whoa, don't say that. I can't get us another place for a while yet."

"I hate him as well."

"I know. Let's not go over all that again. I hate him too. But we have nowhere else to go for now. Can't you just put up with him a while longer for me?"

"Daddy's right. He says you will never find another man like him. You just pick up losers in every corner."

Myrtle caught the spite on her teenager's face. Disappointed, she accepted she may just be right.

She had put her daughter in this situation with an irresponsible alcoholic. But she had no right to speak to her like that.

"Why do you want to pick a fight with me? Is it your hormones? You're stressed. I'm going to ignore that."

"I'm not the only one that hates Marko. Everybody does. It's embarrassing."

"Has he said anything to you? Done anything stupid?"

"Oh yuck, Mum. He is a drunken creep, though. What do you see in him? And you talk about my friends!"

"Severign, calm down. I'm not doing this. Let's get ourselves home and talk about it."

The dyed raven-haired daughter shrugged her shoulders and snuggled up to her mobile phone, muttering to herself.

Eyes firmly on the road, her paint stained knuckles gripped the wheel tensely. Myrtle was at a loss as to why Severign had become bitchier. What was the turning point? Had she missed it somehow? She was such a shy and playful child before. Had she changed since they moved in with Marko?

He was a barometer of extreme emotions from abject joy to total despair and everything else in between. And Marko's relationship with Myrtle was caustic and codependent. Time was she used to relish the challenge. She was his saviour. A six-foot four inch misunderstood Croatian God of testosterone. He carried himself with a remarkable sense of style. They met at his short-lived old bar, Bedlam, behind Harrow Road. He was one of those local legends, whose story was embedded in folklore rather than truth. With no family to speak of in the UK, he came across as somewhat of an enigma. His Croatian roots were all anyone had to go on. Who would dare ask? He could snap and bark if asked directions. The way he ran his business was the same. He only opened when he was in the mood...if he felt like it. He wasn't driven otherwise in order to be consistent. More than anything the bar was an elaborate drinks cabinet for his personal use.

*****

Mother and daughter approached their home in dread. The bar was open. There were patrons spilling onto the street and a rabble-rousing atmosphere evident. Marko's irreverence for business set a precedent.

If the doors opened it was party time. Irregular as his regulars, but usually culminating with a lock-in. Selling drinks by his own measures, inconsistent pricing, shouting at his short-term staff, throwing out and banning the people he didn't like the look of that day...even long standing friends...who always came back. Bedlam. Which is why he named the new bar Bedlam Too.

"Quickly, Sev, get in before he sees us."

Myrtle turned the key in the latch.

"Tch. Why do we have to live here?" sulked Severign. "I wanna go back to Daddy's."

"Get your homework out. The carbonara will be ready soon. I think I've excelled myself this time. I've bought your favourite dessert."

"Listen to them. How am I meant to concentrate with that racket going on?"

"Tell you what, get your homework done, we'll have dinner and we can go and see the new puppies at Auntie Liberty's afterwards. What do you think?"

"I'm not five years old, Mummy. I don't care about...arrgh...what's the point? You don't listen. You never listen," she added, with an all-too familiar irritability to her tone.

"Okay. Forgive me. I've got an idea. How about we go to the pub down Chamberlayne and have a grown up chat. Just you and I?"

"Really? Just us? What about..."

"What about no one. Just you and me, button."

As she stretched out to cuddle her highly strung daughter, Severign shrugged away. "Don't call me that."

"What's the matter, darling...what's with you lately? Tell me...please."

"Nothing. I'm going to my room."

"Hmmm...I'll call you when it's ready."

*****

"Thanks, Mum..." gushed Severign, pushing her bowl away. "That was amazing, your best yet."

Myrtle really was an excellent cook, using only organic ingredients, prepared from scratch.

"I might believe you, had you managed to eat half of it. That'll be your lunch tomorrow."

"I'm just not that hungry. Save the rest for Satan, if he sobers up."

"Babe, you know he has issues. He tries, he really tries. Addiction is a process; we all play our part in it."

"So boring. He's a loser. Another loser stepdad. Thanks."

Bang on cue Marko barged in, steaming.

"Hey, you two, this is very nice...how civilised..."

His coercive stance always began with courteous approach.

And then the switch. His eyeballs bloated with a simmering rage under a furrowed brow. Cheeks sucked in, his body flexed like an animal ready to pounce on its suspecting prey.

"You not going to help me? You can't see that the bar is open? To hell with me? I put this roof over your head and you can't help me?"

"Stop shouting, will you? Take care of the bar yourself. I'm taking Severign out."

"Not tonight…c'mon please," said Marko, his voice softening again. "Come downstairs and help me. It's crazy down there."

"Darling. You've got enough staff on. I've told you before, you have to let me know when you intend to open. I have to make plans," explained Myrtle as calmly as she could.

"Oh? So what if I say the same to you. You live here when I open only, hey? How you like this?"

Marko's voice was getting louder.

Severign got up and pushed passed him indignantly. More in disgust than fear.

"I swear, Marko, I will leave. I mean it. I'm going to leave you. I'm so done with this."

In one movement, Marko wielded Severign's bowl across the room. It smashed heavily onto the wall. He then lifted the glass salad bowl and slammed it onto the table, causing the cutlery to jump.

Myrtle shrieked and Severign ran back into the room. Severign hurled her slim 5'7" frame onto Marko's back and thumped him hard on his ears. Her bulky ring acting as a knuckleduster, drew blood.

"You fucking loser. Leave my mum alone."

"Oh my God. Severign! Don't kill him."

"Bitch. Get off me!"

"You bully. You drunk bastard!"

Severign continued to pummel the brute.

"Get out of here you fuckin' cows. GO."

The entanglement had Myrtle frenziedly trying to prize her daughter from Marko's back, hollering as she did so, while Marko continued to throw anything within his grasp. The bar also sounded like it was being smashed up simultaneously.

They didn't hear the sirens. One officer ran up the stairs into the flat and commanded order. Shocked by the police presence, all three stood to attention. Severign started crying. A policewoman sat mother and daughter down, while Marko was escorted out by another officer.

Myrtle was mortified with a sense of shame and worry. She was concerned about whether any traces of drugs were visible, more than the welfare of her child. When calling social services was mentioned, it hit home.

Severign insisted she was not being abused or in danger and used the situation to her advantage. Her father, Boyd Royle, was her call. Her safe place to be. The balding entrepreneur living in Maida Hill had finally settled down with a steady girlfriend, Marisole Pappa, superficiality personified...fake tits, lip fillers, extensions. Severign disliked her intently.

What did he see in this strumpet? It was as if she didn't know her father at all. Marisole represented everything her rejected mother was not and her presence was a rejection of her as well. She was struggling to figure this out. At least Marisole was self-centred enough not to show any real interest or bore no ill will at the teenager's attention-seeking actions. She could at least vaguely appreciate her for that.

"Dad, Daddy...thank God you picked up. I need help. The police are here."

"What! The police? Are you okay? I'm coming now," panicked Boyd. "They've got him. That loser. He tried to hurt mum. I stopped him."

"You did what? Severign. Severign, where's your mother?"

Passing the phone to her mum and doing her utmost to conceal a wry grin, Severign slumped back in the blue arm chair. The policewoman studied their reactions for motives.

"Boyd. Boyd, we're both alright. Come and pick Sev up as soon as you can. Marko has been an idiot, as fucking usual. Nobody's hurt. Everybody's safe," said Myrtle, failing to put Boyd's mind at rest.

"Everybody's safe. What the hell does that mean? I swear to God if he's touched one hair on my girl's head, I'll kill him. I'll fucking kill you as well."

"Aw, stop with the threats, will you? The police can hear you, you know?"

"I'm deadly serious Myrtle," fumed Boyd, switching to a menacing tone she rarely heard.

"He had better be gone by the time I get there. I'm halfway now. He's a dead man. Don't try to hide anything from me. I wanna know everything. Fuck's sake."

"Here, talk to your father. I've heard enough."

Myrtle shoved the phone at Severign.

"Well, you can't stay here. It isn't advisable...Mrs erm..." The policeman stalled.

"Ms. Sandwell. Myrtle Sandwell."

"Sorry, I'm not looking at my notes. But you'll have to stay somewhere while we get on with things. The bar has been shut down by Noise Pollution for the time being."

"Why? What's gone on?"

"Seems like there was an altercation down there as well as up here. There's been a couple of arrests. I'm afraid that's all I can say for now. Do you have friends, family you can stay with at all? We will need to know where you're staying and how to contact you."

"Things aren't that bad are they officer? Would you guys like some tea? I'll just put a pot on."

"No. Thank you, Ms Sandwell. I would suggest you start putting a bag together for yourself and your daughter."

"We will need to be satisfied that your daughter is not at risk." chipped in the policewoman. "Did you say her father is on his way?"

"Er, yes...she's speaking with him now."

Myrtle was desperately trying to hold her nerve. With each glance at the police officers, she was sure they were scanning the room for clues of drug use. While the paranoia perpetrated her mind, Severign came off the phone.

"Dad's just parking up."

"I can hear him from here."

Boyd's dulcet tones echoed. "What the fuck's gone on here? Yes officer, my daughter is up there can I get past please. Thank you."

Boyd in his Harris Tweed Bakerboy hat was astonished by the carbonara decorated walls.

"It's as bad up here as it is downstairs. What in the fucking world has gone on? Sorry officer."

"Daddy!"

Severign was five years old again.

"Baby girl are you alright, sweetheart?"

"Thank God you're here. Can I come and stay with you? The police say I have to."

"It's your house too, lovely. Stay as long as you want. Did he hurt you? What happened?"

"Excuse me sir, you are?" the policewoman interrupted.

There he was, Boyd Royle, in his jacket-brogues-jeans combo, in her messy flat, how he would gloat...

Myrtle clenched her teeth and clasped her head firmly, facing her Ugg slippered feet, slumped into defeat. What could she say? There was no redeeming the situation.

Let's Hear It For The Boyd

Liberty was full of the joys first thing, her slick coffee machine buzzing in the background.

"Wakey, wakey, sweetpea. Flat white?"

The sofa bed was uncomfortable. The guest room was mid-decoration and the spare had been turned into a dressing room, but Myrtle convinced her bestie otherwise.

A massive yawn and arms outstretched, she peered over to the kitchen island with one eye.

"Shit. What time is it? Wonder if Sev made it to school on time?"

"Check your phone, hun. Here..." Liberty unplugged the mobile from the work top. "Did the dogs keep you awake?"

"Thanks. I cannot tell a lie, the little blighters did keep me awake all night again. Can't stay mad at them for long though. They are adorable."

"Aw, sorry about that. I did wonder. Puppy training classes start soon. Yay."

"Ah, she's in school. Boyd is acting like a father at last. Typical, with only weeks to go in year 10, he's finally doing packed lunches."

"You should've enrolled him in puppy training from the start."

The women rolled about laughing at the idea.

"Pappy school. New business idea there," quipped Myrtle.

"So what are your plans for today?"

"I'm going to see Trotty this afternoon. See if he has any ideas. I think he might know some property people. I'll need a favour. I can't afford an advance or deposit right now. I'm fresh out of funds. If he can't help, that's it for me. I'll have to go back to Winchester with another begging bowl."

"I know what that's like. I have to jump through hoops after a family hand out – painful."

"I would happily jump through as many hoops as they'd like, but my parents desperately want me to move back and bring Severign with me. That will be my only option."

"Can they afford to keep the both of you?"

"Put it this way Libby, if I gave them half a chance, they'd buy me a cottage and even pay for her education. It's not a guess, they've already put it to me, I'm afraid."

"You can't leave London, Myrtle love. Come here, give me a hug, it won't come to that, you'll see."

*****

Myrtle was getting restless, feeling out of sorts with her world. She was homeless, her ex Boyd was trying to isolate her from her daughter, and she had a torrid of emails and calls from the police and social services to follow up. All her belongings were still at the property and Marko just was not cooperating. He wasn't at the flat. The bar was not going to be open for the foreseeable. There were bills outstanding, invoices from beer suppliers or energy companies. She wasn't certain how much she was responsible for. If she turned up at the flat, would bailiffs be waiting? Or worse still Marko himself, she wondered?

Owing money when you weren't making any was the worst. She just wanted to run from her responsibilities but knew the only way to make this mess go away was money. Dare she go cap in hand to Boyd? The idea that after all this time he would take sole custody of Severign filled her with dread. The battles she waged with him and his partying habit while their daughter was a toddler were firmly planted in her memory. She gasped as the wretched questions roamed her mind relentlessly.

When she and Boyd first met, he was a courier for a record company. He had lied to her and implied he owned both the indie company and the courier firm. He went to all the major raves and festivals, which he insisted he reclaimed as business expenses. She was his plus one until she fell pregnant. Then the full extent of the truth came to light. The indie record label was a complete fallacy. The strand of truth was the courier firm, a family business bequeathed by Boyd's father, but owned and run by his brother, Cecil Royle.

Boyd's lack of interest meant that he was bought out and persuaded to take a courier job on his family firm's payroll, Royle Lineage. When Myrtle met him, he was at the tail end of his pay-off. When it came to the crunch she realised that even his flat share was a rental and he didn't own that either. His flatmate was not helping him pay off the mortgage as she was led to believe. She was not going to be allowed to move in with him after all. She too was in a flat share.

Cecil had the fortitude to hold back some of the money from the firm as a contingency measure for his brother's predictable liability. Graciously, he had reinvested a share back in the business tied up in a property for Myrtle and Boyd to live in on the border of Kensal Rise and Harlesden. The agreement being that any profit share went back into the business and the property. Boyd had little choice in the matter. There was a baby on the way.

As the years rolled on, Boyd started neglecting his parental duties. He had successfully acquired new business to Royle Lineage that included introducing a forward thinking IT system, which was their catalyst for expansion. It was then that he was motivated by ambition. He followed his brother's lead; became more interested and took on the air of a businessman. At the realisation of his profit share he discarded his Hawaiian shirts, thong shoes and neckerchiefs for high end, dapper accessories. Unfortunately, with this reinvention came women. The shiny, glossy kind of women, whose standard attire was directed at exploiting their obvious assets, paid for or natural.

By the time Severign was four years old, Myrtle had to make the biggest decision of her life, and left Boyd. It was a wrench. Ever since she had been moving from one flat to the other and moving in with one boyfriend or another.

Boyd paid for Severign's welfare, but to keep that cost down he insisted on having access to her on a regular basis and most of the school holidays. He could afford to look after them, but made it difficult by paying just over enough child support to keep it from the family courts. Myrtle faced her Hobson's choice on numerous occasions. She knew that giving Severign up was never an option, not even to her parents in sunny Winchester.

From her pepper white Mini Clubman, an old 40th birthday present from her parents, Myrtle called Boyd on the phone on her way to meet Trotty.

"Boyd. Listen. We need to talk like adults about what we're going to do, for Severign's sake. Please don't talk over me or talk down to me."

"Charming. Have I said anything yet?"

"When's good for a catch up?"

"Let me call you back. Severign's alright where she is with me. I am her father."

"I didn't say she wasn't. Let's not do this? This was what I didn't want. Stating the bloody obvious."

"You are the one that has got into this mess. Not me. You can't blame me."

"It's not a blame game. I thought we could talk and see what we could come up with until I sort things out."

"Well I don't know just now. Like I said, I will get back to you. Severign's alright where she is with me. She gets fed and watered. She's doing her homework. You've got nothing to worry about. I've been dropping and picking her up from school on time."

"Yes. I know. I appreciate that. Thank you. You won't have to for much longer. I'm going to sort something out."

"I'm sure you will. But she's not going anywhere near any more of your deadbeat boyfriends. The girl needs stability. You should be putting her first."

"Like you? Hightailing it with your flashy tarts? Where were you when..."

"Not that again. Look I'll call you. Yeah?"

"Hmmm." Myrtle was teetering on an emotional edge again. "I'm trying my best. Get her to call me. No, tell her I'll call her this evening."

She muttered under her breath "cunt," as she rang off. Boyd looked down at his mobile and mumbled "cunt" too.

*****

Outside the Coffee Hype cafe in Golborne Road, Myrtle offloaded on a cross legged, Trotty.

"I still can't believe this has happened. My phone hasn't stopped going. I've got emails demanding money. That fucking arsehole has forwarded my details to some of the suppliers. I need to find somewhere for me and my daughter to live. I'll have to get a proper job. I'll have to turn down that contract I told you about, for the children's book illustrations because I don't have the time and there won't be enough money. Liberty's sofa is hurting my back and her puppies howl like babies at night. If I don't sort myself out soon, I'll lose Severign and have to go back to my parents. For God's sake, I am middle aged with onset menopause. What the actual fuck. My life's over, Trots."

Trotty's comedic exasperated expression, lightened up the rant. Myrtle could tell she was setting him up for a repost.

"Ding, Dong. What did you say about Liberty's puppies?"

"Hahaha, she has a fine pair, but they are rather feral, yet to be housetrained."

"Darling...you're so funny even in a crisis. I'm going to miss that."

"Bless you darling. There's me going on and you've got your Biennale to think about."

"What can I do? How can I help? I've always thought Marko was a loser, but he's really dropped you in it, the dodgy pillock."

"I don't know, I don't know Trots. Do you know anyone that has small flat to let or a share, without some massive deposit or reference? It's a big ask. I'm running out of options."

"Hmmm. I've been thinking about that. Anyway. I have a proposition for you, but I'm just rethinking it..."

"Oh, Trotsta. Anything. I'll consider anything right now."

"Please, darling, don't beg so. It's doesn't become you."

"Trotty, drop the Noël Coward routine, please, I'm fucking homeless. Seriously, though, hun, anything that can get me out this jam..."

"Meet me tonight, at my Westbourne place. You remember where it is?"

* * * * *

"Who's the boy, Severign?"

"No one Daddy. Just some boy."

"Don't get cute with me, young lady. I was a teenager myself once and the dance is the same. Tell me, or I'll ask him myself."

Boyd got pretty stern in his BMW, the motor left running.

"I swear, Dad, if you say anything to him?"

"Look, Sev, I don't mind who you hang out with, I'm not like your mother, but the last thing I want is you getting into trouble while you're living with me. I'll never hear the end of it. Is he your boyfriend?"

"No, he's in my friendship group. We all hang out sometimes, that's all."

"Okay, I get it. Why don't you invite your 'friendship group' over? Get some pizzas..."

"Can I have them over? Will you be out?"

"Hang on a minute. That is not what I meant."

"Tch...boring."

"Wait. Wait a minute. Look, how do you feel about coming to live with me full time, especially starting your GCSEs next term?"

"Can I? Are you serious?"

"Of course I'm serious. My little baby girl is a young lady now. You'll be off soon and you'll forget about yer 'ole man."

Severign leant across the passenger seat of the car and kissed her father on the cheek. Slumping back smugly she responded...

"His name is Archie, but that's all I'm saying right now. He's a friend of Dande's son."

"She still knocking about?"

"Who, Dande?"

"Yeah, she's married to that DJ Eli Stefano, isn't she?"

"Think so, dunno. I met him at the workshop with Mummy."

"So your mother knows him?"

"No...don't think so anyway?"

"Has she met the boy, Sev? Be straight with me?"

"What's all this, Dad? It's no big deal. Mum hasn't met all my friends. She's an embarrassment."

"Behave. I'm not your mother's biggest fan, but that kind of talk is out of order."

"You know she is..."

"Oi, look, keep the 'living with me' thing under wraps for now. Give me a bit of time to work on her. She won't be happy, so when we get in, put your phone away, charge it or something, just for an hour and do your homework or whatever it is. Give me a bit of peace. We can talk about stuff over the weekend. Daddy loves ya."

Severign glared at him.

Open Sashimi

Just a few days after the affray at Bedlam Too, Environmental Health sought a warrant to close down the bar for good via a public disorder order. It was going into receivership and Marko was past caring about how much money he was about to lose...or owed.

For Myrtle, time was now of the essence. A removal van on limited funds – i.e. a favour from someone - needed to be hastily arranged to collect her personal effects, including her wardrobe of vintage and haute couture pieces she had been collecting since she was a size zero in her twenties.

She had shoes, hats and wigs too, all stuck inside the flat. She had to get everything packed up before the bailiffs seized control of the property and changed the locks.

Myrtle tried in vain to organise a midnight flit on the Thursday, which ended up being a Friday afternoon for all the neighbours to see. She underestimated how many personal belongings were in the furnished flat. So, help was enlisted and Trotty and Boyd tolerated each other for a few hours while helping mother and daughter.

Boyd packed his car with Severign's excess. The rest was bound for their new address in Westbourne Grove. Boyd was screwing over Myrtle's decision to move into Trotty's flat. It still didn't sound like a permanent place for his daughter. Once again, he thought his ex was forcing him to entrust his girl under the care of some bloke he barely knew.

Boyd was once enamoured by Myrtle's private school accent, but the novelty soon wore off. Bringing up their baby exhausted their starkly differing outlooks.

He mocked Trotty and Myrtle as they had 'a posh off' with their polite wittering on.

Severign wanted to live with her father but couldn't resist the pull of the Westbourne Grove first floor flat. She had blagged the double bedroom with ensuite bathroom. Myrtle had trumped Boyd without even knowing it.

Before they took off in a convoy, Severign made a point of jumping in with her father for the ride.

"I'll come with you Daddy."

"Just follow us, then, we'll lead the way." ordered Trotty.

"If that's not everything, I couldn't care less. Let's just go. I want to get away from here as soon as possible and never turn back. Ugh!"

The short five-minute journey from Kensal Rise could be a mission, often taking 20 or more minutes, especially mid to late afternoon when school's out. The spiritual home of the 'Chelsea Tractor', alongside the black cabs and Übers clogging up the non-pedestrianised, tourist-filled streets, in perpetuum.

Working for Dande was a Godsend. She had generously loaned out her furniture truck to Myrtle, who was now adept at sneaky manoeuvres in the light HGV, having driven it on deliveries here and there.

"Whoa! Less Stirling Moss, more Kate Moss, darling...last thing I need is whiplash," moaned Trotty.

"Sorry, darling. Forgot you were there. I was in the zone."

"Don't talk. Keep focused. Let's get there in one piece."

"Darling, I can't believe you're letting us live in your flat. I just want to say how grateful I am. I'll always remember this. Will you stay for supper? I'll make something exotic for us while Severign's at her father's."

"I thought they were following behind us?"

"Yes. She's dropping her stuff off in her room first then staying with her father until I get the place in order."

"In that case don't cook. Let's order some sushi. I want to run a few things by you in private if that's okay?"

"Sounds ominous. But anything for you, 'favourite person'...just going to pull up over here."

Myrtle sang, gingerly climbing the pavement lip.

Boyd eyed the van in the distance, parking just a few cars behind. Jumping out, he helped Severign grab her bin liner possessions and laid them up the path.

"See you've landed on your feet again?" he scoffed at Myrtle.

"Just leave her things there. We'll take care of them."

"Mummy, can I show Daddy my room?"

A firm "No," came the reply.

"I have a right to see where my daughter is going to live, you know?"

"Daddy, leave it. It's okay."

"Well we're hardly squatting." Myrtle gestured at the grand Regency pillars of the entrance.

"Come on, let's have a clean break, no fighting," interjected Trotty.

"Is that everything, Sev? You heading back with Daddy?"

"Erm, yes. I can stay if you want, though?"

"No, no darling. Come here, give me a kiss and hurry along. I'll have the place nice for you before you move in. Now thank Uncle Trotty, he's been a lifesaver."

"Thanks, Trotty. I can't wait to move in."

"You're most welcome my sweetheart. I'll see you soon. Give us a hug."

"Go on, give him a hug."

As Severign and Boyd drove off, Trotty made some calls to a couple of local 'hands' from Portobello market, to help unload the van. They made light work of Myrtle's chattels.

*****

The beautifully furnished study was an oasis of calm that belied the untidy unpacked materials in the hallway.

Myrtle and Trotty, now waiting over an hour for their sushi delivery, were horizontal in fatigue and awash with red wine.

"Myrtle. Can I be straight with you?"

"Yes, of course, go on?"

"Do you know you must have run up a tab of over £2k over the years. I've let you pay me back in dribs and drabs, but you've been nowhere near covering it."

"2k? Wow. Is it that much? Suppose it must be about that. I will pay you back. All of it."

"No, no, no, listen. Don't interrupt. This is important. I've been thinking...howabout...I wipe the slate clean for you. Originally, I suggested you pay a minimal rent including bills, but I'm also going to waiver that for you."

"Trotty? You can't do that?"

"Ssshhh. Listen. It's not that simple. I'm proposing you act as caretaker for this property in my place. My family will never sell it. But we have responsibilities and I've been on the shitty end of that, because I chose to be an artist. The irony being that my Great, Great somebody was bequeathed it as a gambling debt settlement along with some very fine art. I won't say any more than that. I digress. What I'm getting at, is you will have to help honour the upkeep of the property, let builders in and assist the tenants and estate agents. Basically, earn your lodgings as a kind of facilities manager. I think you're up to it. Is this a fair deal?"

"Oh gosh. Trotty, you are full of surprises. Of course I can do that. I am terribly grateful, I can hardly say no?"

"I sort've got the idea knowing I was going to be in South Africa. What do you say? You'll do it?"

"Hmmm, it's come as a bit of a shock. Before I commit, will you help me with it first. I just need to garner some idea of what I'm getting into, really. I have Severign to consider.

"Darling. It's a piece of piss. How long have you known me? Do I look that busy? Hahaha."

"Do you really want me to answer that?"

"Actually, could you answer the door? Think that's the sushi."

The colourful array of Asian cuisine, the odour of the sea, filled the atmosphere.

"Crack open another bottle, Myrtle. Grab a white if you prefer."

"I'm red 'til I'm dead...you know that, sushi or no."

"You philistine."

They continued to plough through the Japanese seafood, chuckling as they did so, embarrassed by their hunger fuelled noshing.

"Erm, darling there is one other thing I need to float by you. Don't take offence. I'm just asking. I would never put you in the way of any danger or..."

"What the fuck are you asking me now, Trots?"

"Sorry, sorry. I'll talk to you another time. It's a bit much. I love these, have a bite."

"Yummy. Dee-lish. No, darling, tell me everything while I'm still in shock position."

"Err, okay. I've been meaning to run this by you. You need dosh, don't you? Lots of it? Don't answer, that was rhetorical. I know your position. I trust you, Myrt...and it is because I trust you that I want to put this proposition to you."

Myrtle froze with a half-bitten California roll between her teeth.

"I want you to take over my patch for me. Run it until I get back. You know all my clients. You've seen how I conduct myself. Could you? Would you do it?"

"Whoa. Trotty, Trot-trot, noooooo. What, supplying all your clients? You have got to be kidding me?"

"Yes. I am deadly serious. I'm not getting any younger and I doubt I'll ever get the chance of a Biennale again. It's my last opportunity to achieve my artistic goal. But I can't afford to lose my patch. You're an artist. You understand."

"But you went to Goldsmiths. You've had exhibitions, reviews, you've shown in galleries, had an agent? This isn't your last opportunity at all."

"Now you sound just like my family."

"Sorry... I don't understand."

"Look. Think about it. You'll be living here rent free. You will earn most of my takings. It will be a chance for you to save up and move out in a year's time. You could save enough for a deposit even. Pay back that five grand you owe your parents. I've already written off two grand for you. Think about it? I will need an answer soon."

"Well, I was just mulling over sitting in this flat running the whole shebang. Then you drop this bombshell."

"I know. I know. I'm sorry. But I haven't much time. The festival season and holidays are coming up and my clients need a reliable hook up. I'm going to have to recommend someone else or do some deal. But I've built this up and I'm loathed to toss it away just like that. Like I said. You're the one person in my life I trust to run it and then hand it back in one piece."

"Brrr...," shuddered Myrtle. "I can't eat anymore."

The rest of the evening flew by as the two friends chatted away. A few more bottles of Rioja and a line or two of finest uncut Colombian marching powder. Myrtle with a sideways glance, wondering what new mess she had got herself into. Was Trotty such a good egg as first thought? She was in a tight spot. Her first night in this gorgeous new home and she would not be able to sleep, though she was very, tired. The over-whelming issue was how to say 'no' politely.

To her mind, when someone has stretched out a kind hand to rescue you from impending dire straits, you are, inextricably, honour bound to return the favour.

As she lay on her back looking at the intricate plasterwork of the ceiling rose, she wondered what the street value of sleep was. Quite certain that she might never know what it is to experience that again.

Small Matters

Over the summer months, weather allowing, Boyd and his Greek Cyrpiot mate Georgiou would knock up a midweek barbecue. Georgiou's speciality, handcrafted wine sausages were the main event.

The guys used to get their children together when they were little, however these days it was just the two of them. Georgiou's wife refused to hang out with anymore of Boyd's conveyor belt of colourful girlfriends. Their teenager's rare appearance took the form of them dipping in and out with little or no interest in the BBQ except to pick...and ask for money for a takeaway.

The bros would spend the sunset in the outhouse at the back of the garden smoking joints and swilling cans of beer until nightfall.

This was one such evening. The recent upheaval of Boyd's ex Myrtle the number one topic. Unsurprising, as he had been slagging off Marko for some time.

"So you're sure Myrtle's not, you know, doing the naughty with this Trotty fella? I don't really get that friendship mate?"

"Well, you never know with her. He's one of them trustafarians. Never done a hard day's work in his life. You know, you've met him. Can't figure them out myself. But it's that Marko that worries me, G. There's all kinds of bother going on since that bar closed down and Myrtle is well and truly caught up in it."

"He's a wally. No disrespect, but she can't half pick 'em. So, how's Sev dealing with it all?"

"Gawd. It's all happening now, mate. She's 16 in

September...going on sixty. I cannot tell a lie, I'm out of me depth. She's been hanging round some boy lately. I don't know how to best handle it."

"Got one of my own, as you know. Like, every night she fights with her sisters and her mother. Luckily Maria can handle her, most of the time I just leave them to holler it out. It's mental, I tell ya."

"Maria is a goodun. I'd never go out with posh totty again. You think it'd be easier, but they come fully loaded with 'first world problems', mate. Yup, you did alright with Maria."

Georgiou nodded in agreement and then passed the much needed spliff to his mate. They didn't notice Severign coming towards them. She had caught some of what was said.

"Daddy!"

"Quick, hide it..."

Boyd panicked trying to put out the spliff and stash the paraphernalia behind the cans of beer.

"Sev, what have I told you about sneaking around up here when George is over?"

"Cut it out, pops. I know what you do up in here," she chuckled.

"Oi." Boyd stood up to walk towards her. "What's up?"

"Nothing, just wondering if I could pop out for a bit. I'll be back by 10.30pm – just for an hour?"

"No darling. It's a school night. It's not me, it's your mother. If she gets wind..." Severign looks over at Georgiou for approval.

"Anna goes out midweek sometimes. You trust her don't you Uncle G?"

Awkward.

"Well yeah, we do Sev, but she's older than you and besides, we know the company she keeps. They come round to ours all the time. Some of them never leave."

"Don't put him on the spot girl! Rude. These are my

rules. I said no and that's the end of it."

"It's not fair," pouted Severign, turning and stomping back to the house before an abrupt stop. "Can my friends come over, like you promised?"

"Yes, we'll work something out. Not tonight, though. Now leave me in peace luv."

"Go back to your toot, hahaha."

"Ooof, you're in trouble, mate. She's growing up fast."

"Into quite the handful. Love her to bits but I'm losing the will..."

*****

With only the glimmer of the phone light, Severign curled up in bed, chatting to Archie.

"They treat me like a kid. I've got Mummy on one side and Daddy on the other, using me as a pawn in their parenting game. It's like I'm waving to them saying I'm right here in front of you. I've got a brain, yeah? I understand everything you're saying. Ask me what I think, yeah?"

"They're all like that. It's what they do. I've only got my mum to deal with and that's plenty, believe me."

"Sorry, I keep forgetting that. It must be hard not having a dad. But then again, with my one, the only nice things he does are just to get one up on my Mum. I have to play it to my advantage."

"I know, they haven't a clue. Mum's so desperate for me to be a scientist or something, she thinks she's been buying me 'nuclear workshop' equipment, but at least the kit helps get some phat chops out of my studio."

"Hahaha. That's sad. She still can't tell you're doing music? You're evil Archie."

"Bae, it's not about science and technology, it's the fact that she's hell bent on keeping me out of music altogether. Trying to get me to enjoy Classical and Opera.

Listening to Radio 4 rather than 6 Music. It's weird. I don't understand it."

"The more she does it, hey?"

"Sending you the link of today's mix, yeah?"

"Have you done one about me yet?"

"Yeah. Chill. It's coming."

"Miss you, bae."

"Me too."

"Guess what, I caught Daddy by the out house having a toot with his mate. It was perfect timing, so I asked him if I could have friends round. I'm normally only allowed one friend at a time, like some play date. Maddening. Anyway, he says I can. So, I was thinking we could get the group together and sit up in the out house? What d'ya think?"

"Well, I ain't got nowhere for us to go and it will change things up from Bertie's place. Yeah, nice one."

"Anyway, I'm 16 in a few months so then I can do what I like."

"How's this gonna work when you move back in with your mum? Will you get to your Dad's as often?"

"There's going to be some changes. But Mummy is always out and Daddy and his girlfriend go out every weekend fortnight. Yes, gonna be changes. Watch me."

"I can talk. Look at me, I'm like a nearly 18 year old prisoner in my mother's boot camp."

"I haven't met your mother yet, hahaha...jokes...I'm sure she loves you to bits, Arch, give her a break."

"Let's change the subject. Download that link I sent you."

* * * * *

Three weeks since the flat move, Myrtle had managed to rearrange the furniture in situ and leave some of her own things in storage. The kitchen, she believed was the heartbeat of any home and wanted to get this right. It had a stainless range cooker with brass knobs, barely used. She gave the empty cupboards, tiles, the sink and marble surface a good going over using vinegar and soda, under Severign's supervision. It took twice as long and double the effort as a result.

She raised an eyebrow when she noticed the grey dust was splattered with a conspicuous white substance. There was no escaping Trotty's voice in her head. Despite not having agreed to anything yet, bit by bit he acted presumptuously, showing her the ropes when they hung out.

Her options were closing in rapidly, unable to communicate with Marko and sort through the mountain of red tape concerning Bedlam Too.

It was Trotty who reminded her to seek help from a women's refuge charity for guidance as referred by the police. An idea she had dismissed out of hand initially. She was involved in a fracas, not a victim of domestic abuse and didn't need this kind of service.

She was not one of those people. As it turned out, the organisation referred her to another service for financial advice and guidance. They were able to help her write a legally binding letter admonishing her of all the bar's liabilities. Myrtle felt some small relief knowing that this letter was pending. Marko and his shenanigans were off her back for this spell.

Once again, she had Trotty to thank. Myrtle started getting some ingredients ready to make flapjacks. A glass of red to hand while she did so. Something healthy, she thought, for Severign to snack on that would, hopefully, smell luscious throughout the flat.

*****

London is a joy to behold when the sun casts light and

shadow over its architectural wonders. Interspersed with a cornucopia of foliage and great parks it espouses a sense of halcyon days to come; the music of birdsong hyped by a chorus of whirring cyclists, traffic and jostling commuters.

Myrtle offered to take Liberty and the twins (the pooches she named Justin and Lisa) for a Hampstead Heath walk. They were like sisters from another mother. Both blonde, taller than average, still raving on the house music scene with their middle age peers. Theirs was a facade that beheld self-assured, confident, articulate women. Beneath that, not so much.

Aside from their red wine and coke habit, they spent many hours on an endless spree of discovering new holistic treatments: mani-pedi, hair colouring and fortnightly back massages. Once in a while a spa date, a period of yoga sessions. They decided, as they often did, to wear similar outfits. Short jean skirts and flip flops, white broderie anglaise tops and huge shades...their conditioned, but wispy locks tied back.

"I live for flip flop days, but bad idea for this walk."

"I know, I forget I have to chase after the little blighters."

"They are so cute and getting so big. What's their full size going to be and can you manage two?"

"I know, they're eating me out of house and home. I have no idea what my life was like before them. As a breed, pugs grow to about 12 inches high...I think...I bloody hope."

"How's Freddy adjusting to them?"

"He's getting there, now, haha. It hasn't been easy. You know his dad's just had a stroke? He's booking flights for him and his brother to go to Guyana to see him."

"Oh poor darling. Didn't his mum die last year? I mean, all so soon..."

"Yes, I know. I feel for him. He's not saying much, but I think he's coping. Such a shame for his dad."

"They were alright with you, weren't they?"

"Oh, Freddy's parents have been a joy. They made such a fuss of me. They were so proud of him and his achievements. I wish I could go with him, but the twins... too soon to leave them in kennels. Don't think Freddy understands, though."

"Don't go saying, they're just like kids, because my darling let me assure you, they are certainly not."

"Well, I don't know how you manage, darling. What's Severign up to?"

Ever since we left Bedlam Too, she's spent more time with her father than with me," sighed Myrtle. "I literally can't keep up. Apparently, I have to share the responsibility more equally with Boyd because I can't be trusted to protect her. Fucking Marko, he's wrecked my life."

"Darling, I know...could have been so much worse."

"Huh, I've barely told you the half of it, hun."

"Tell you what, fill me in later...we can grab a cider on the way back. Let's just enjoy the sunshine."

"Actually, there's something I need to run by you and it doesn't involve Marko. But this time it feels like I've fallen from the frying pan into a vat of hot oil."

"Myrtle, darling," whispered a concerned Liberty. "What's happened? Let's go sit down."

Trying to create modesty where there was none with unforgiving denim, the women sat at opposites, cradling a dog each between their thighs to spare their blushes.

"Look, you can't say anything to anyone. Not anyone. Not even Freddy. Okay?"

"Shit. Myrtle, you're scaring me now."

"It's Trotty," she began.

"Oh my God, he's finally told you...he's in love with you."

"If only! No. He's put me in a bit of a position and I just can't see a way out."

Myrtle explained her plight. Her fears, her circumstances. Most of all she was desperate for a second opinion on Trotty. Had she got him all wrong? Had he been subtlety coercing her all along? The five, six, seven or so years, in which they had built a genuine friendship. Was it all a sham? She hated herself for doubting his sincerity. There was a feeling of betrayal just to hear herself say it out loud. Liberty, however, held a more pragmatic view.

"I can see why you're thinking the worst, but Trotty isn't like that. He's an artist, for God's sake darling. He comes from a good family. He's not grooming you. Gosh. Noooooo!"

"I don't know what to think. I haven't really slept since."

"Look, it's just for the one year, you said? You already know his clients? You get to make a bit of money that will get you out of a hole. So take it. See it as your own Biennale. One year will fly by at little or no risk."

"If I get caught, Libby? I've got to think of Sev, no matter what."

"Darling, we do it all the time anyway. We buy it, share it, sell a gram or two at a party, a sit up, don't we?"

"Yeah."

"We've been doing it for years and years, decades even, and nothing's ever happened. So, for one year you're doing that bit more. I'm sure you can refine his operation with his clients?"

"You make it sound so simple."

"What's the alternative?"

"He might throw us out and slap a two grand bill on top of what I owe him. It could get nasty. What if he turns? Haven't really seen that side of him."

"That's because he's not like that. Trotty just isn't that sort. You've been watching too many thrillers."

"Tch, tch, tch, tch, tch, how did I get here, Lib? What the fuck, hey?" she sighed.

Tufts of grass between fingers, dog leads on wrist, Liberty tried to move in closer to her bestie.

"Aw, love. It seems bad because you've been coming at it negatively. It's only for one year. I'll even help you if you like?"

"No, I can't expect you to do that."

"What is it you're really scared of? Trotty? The police?"

"Just a small matter...I've had enough of dealings with the rossers as it is."

"We could bring the dogs with us on our rounds. The sniffer dogs will be distracted by them and not us. What do you think?"

"Great. Hmmm..."

"Who's going to stop us two? Pull us over for a stop and search? Haha...we're just two dizzy, blonde West London chicas. As long as we don't drink, I know that's going to be the hardest part, nudge-nudge, but we won't get stopped, darling. What's more I am absolutely sure Trotty knows people. He can call in a favour, can't he?"

"You've got the dizzy blonde part right. I wish I'd never asked. But thank you. You treasure. Love you."

Class Rules

The white facade of the Covent Garden building was flooded with crimson and yellow images projected above the red-carpet entrance to the flagship shop launch. The paparazzi were outside waiting for the A-listers to show – all fashionably late, of course. Their flash bulbs added to the electricity in the atmosphere. False alarms of whoops, cheers and screams rang out at the arrival of social media doyens and influencers by adoring fans waiting outside.

Trotty was wearing green and red striped slacks, an open shirt, a mustard scarf and matching linen jacket, holding hands with his current favourite accessory, Myrtle. She was looking especially elegant against the lights, in a light silk tunic dress in some indecipherable muted colour. Swinging her pashmina against her long, tanned, middle-aged legs, still holding up well in a pair of Gina heels.

As they gave their names to the door people, Trotty took command and produced his sketch book and an art pouch of charcoals and oil crayons. They were swiftly ushered in, but once inside they were forced to stop a moment to take pictures against the logo backdrop for press and PR. They milked the opportunity to strike a pose, the same ones they always did at these events.

The champagne flow followed by a nose up in the washroom, then another. As more champagne flowed, they set to work.

Heavily dramatised greetings and disguised camaraderie hid fiddly handshakes with wraps, some slipped into back pockets, and re-up orders whispered into ears. A universally recognised routine, played out on international party circuits, effortlessly adopted by the initiated from NYC, Miami to Ibiza and London to LA...et al.

The buzz reached dizzying heights as the stardust sprinkle at the arrival of an international top model made her appearance. One superstar DJ, a Hollywood A-lister and pop star. Lapped up by the media, trending, online e-zines and cult mags. This was a once or twice a month gig for the likes of Trotty, but part of the daily grind for those star guests.

Like any successful brand, this was slick marketing and commerce of the most delicate kind. The communication between supplier, dealer and end user like gossamer wings over wifi. You could barely see it to the touch.

"How fucking good's this party, Myrt."

"I know. Can't believe she said hello to me. Me! Huhuh."

"Well, think we've done enough mingling. We need to leave. Shame really."

"Do we have to? All this champers, think that waiter likes me."

"You say that every time. Come along dear, we have to go. Now."

"Spoil sport."

Myrtle was reluctant, but her heels were already planning respite ahead of her.

"Let's get this cab to the car."

"Aww. Feeling slightly tipsy. The bubbly always tickles."

"Love a double drop off in town like this. Less to do rest of the week. The theatre lot got theirs and the launch was timely. If only every day could be this easy."

"In my case a relief to get away from the domestic grind."

"You recognise everyone now don't you? My people?"

"Your people who are very soon to become my people, hic."

"Oh gawd, dear. Let's get you home. Now where did we park again?"

*****

Another hazy afternoon and a mani-pedi booked for two, Myrtle met Liberty in the Portobello Road salon, glugging down the single complimentary glass of Prosecco as the women chatted in code.

"Lib, my love, were you serious about, you know, helping me out if I agreed to take on Trotty's stuff?"

With a slow turn of the head, Liberty chose to respond with eyeball to eyeball contact at her pal, nodding in agreement.

"I think I'm going to do it. I'm going in, hun. God help us. I'm going to do it. I'll tell him tonight."

"Honestly, darling. You'll be fine. It's just for a year and you've got me onside. Tell him tonight. Once you've committed you'll feel lighter. Then you'll just get on with it. The time will fly by. Promise."

"Thank goodness for you, Lib. Please stay close, it's going to be a bumpy ride."

Trotty was back from an action-packed festival and notably in recovery.

Myrtle admired her manicured nails, holding the

mobile as she spoke to Trotty on loud speaker from the flat.

"Hi, Snotty. Still fragile, are we?"

"Oh, darl, never again. It was a blast, but I'm struggling. ODing on Lemsips I swear to you...I'm too old for this. How everyone else manages I'll never know. It was relentless. Wish you'd been there."

"Yeah, I wish too. But after all this house moving, I hadn't got the energy for Glasto. Severign has settled in now. The flats looking nicer. Come round. She's at her father's later."

"Oh, hun, can we do another night?"

"Erm, no. We have to talk and if I don't do it now I never will."

"Is this what I think you're talking about? Are you going to...for me?"

"Hmmm. Well, yes. But let's talk face to face."

"Be right there. That was the cure I needed," responded Trotty, with a new reserve of energy. "What time?"

Severign was patted off again to her father who was waiting outside.

"Shall I wait 'til Trotty comes, Mummy? I seem to keep missing him lately?"

"Don't worry, I'll organise a date for us soon, he's always asking after you. Have you got everything?"

"I'm going to Daddy's down the road, not the moon! What time's he coming? I can get Daddy to come back later?"

"Darling, please. He's just back from Glastonbury he's probably not going to make it. The last thing he needs is a pesky teenager on his case. C'mon, stop stalling."

"I'm not thirteen y'know. See ya."

"Kiss?"

"Tch. See ya. Love ya." Severign trundled down the communal staircase in her uniform pastel shade baggy sweatpants and hoodie.

Outside, car engine running, a bewildered Boyd looks up at the seemingly void Regency windows. What goes on up there? He should be allowed to see where his only child lives. After all, when the shit hits the fan, who's she going to call? That Marko business was the last straw. Although Severign was his responsibility, he was frustrated at having to manage Myrtle's mistakes as a matter of course.

In the meantime, he had no control over her poor decisions. He had enough to think about with the family courier business Royle Lineage.

"Hi Daddy."

"Sev. How is it up there, girl?"

"The flat? Hmmm...it's nice."

"You happy there? You'd tell me?"

"Daddy, stop fussing. I have an ensuite. Plus, anything is better than Marko' place."

"I'm so sorry I left you there. I should've put a stop to it sooner."

"Yes, you should have. But that's done now. I'm happy where I am and I'm happy at yours too. What's for dinner?"

"It's not just mine, it's your home too. Whenever you're ready to make it a permanent fixture, just say the word?"

"You know I would in a heartbeat, but Mummy would have a meltdown...she needs me. She won't admit it."

"Marisole is in, she's cooking summat."

Severign groaned rudely and reassumed the transfixed position to her WhatsApp chat with Archie over the journey - all 10/15 minutes of it.

It wasn't until gone nine that Trotty made a bedraggled, unshaven appearance which had Myrtle's nerves holding out for the last couple of hours.

After supplying him with detox tea and a large Bloody Mary with all the trimmings, they assumed the position across the giant pouffe in the study. The mood resembled that of a war chest meeting. General Trotty giving the orders and setting out the tried and tested strategy to yield successful net results.

How the gear would be supplied, but not by whom.

What to do in any given circumstance upon receipt of the gear.

How to divide up the materials and when.

Dos and Don'ts.

Her infantry would be dropped off at his Battersea home. There was a workman's entrance outside for legitimate deliveries. It was a discreet box with a six-digit code. In it was where she would collect the goods and the little resealable plastic bags.

He advised her to use her own art portfolio to put the stuff in before taking it to her car. No one else had the code except her. She was to make her collection any time after Tuesday mornings. Never at the same time points. Either 10am one week 12 noon the next, 4pm another. Always before 6pm. No one would see her as the 8ft hedgerow hid her movements.

One shelf in the study at the Westbourne Grove flat was not all it seemed. Inlaid on the shelf was a digital scale. Trotty had built the LED reader into the shelf and covered it with a pile of reading materials he was certain no one would want to ever lift up or read, including 20 copies of the Watch-Tower, the Jehovah's Witness magazines. They were yellowing and dog-eared. He would say they belonged to the last tenant, not that anyone ever really came to the flat.

As Myrtle anticipated, the enormity of the task ahead began to dawn on her. It was beginning to hit home literally. She held her nerve by reminding herself why she was here. A decent place, a stop gap, for herself and child to live rent free, a regular income that would see her straight and able to afford to plant stable roots going forward a year from now. She contemplated the risks, but realistically any likelihood of getting caught were slim to none based on her peers. Everyone she had heard about in trouble generally got off with a caution or warning. With one exception, a young, amateur, stupidly served up for the first time at Glasto and as a result was imprisoned. Even he was a friend of a friend of a friend.

Apart from her bust ups with Marko, these were her only run-ins with the law. If she or Marko had been tested for drug use after one of their domestics, they would have been banged up for certain.

She found focusing on giving her daughter an unforgettable Sweet Sixteen party and extra school tuition enough of a motivation to keep going.

Trotty had omitted to share the main upside of his proposition. He encouraged her to gain new clients she could trust to serve up an extra ounce too. That proverbial 'difficult second ounce'.

She was to hold dinner parties and organise outings or attend events in groups and be the sole provider of the fun bags within said group. That included festivals, a girls night in, mothers who lunched, anything that included the freely flowing imbibe of red wine. Orders increased under the influence. She knew who he meant. The fine lining demographic. Herself, a fully paid up member.

Trotty continued his sermon and issued a stark warning.

"This game comes with its own risks...obvious risks. But having done this for a couple of decades, I know that my client's discretion is why this vocation has been a successful one for me. I have kept to these strict guidelines which actually work. You must adhere to them. I hope you understand. There are severe consequences for all of us if you do not."

Myrtle nodded her head like a toddler being lifted a penance from the naughty step.

"Never ever take anyone to the pick up point or send them in your place. It is better to be late or miss a delivery than that. Okay? Next, should the worst happen, and it won't - feign ignorance, say nothing or blame it on a one-night stand. You'll get bail. And then I'll make sure you get the best lawyer. You will be covered, you'll be okay. But only if you say nothing at all."

"Oh, you're scaring me." Myrtle bit her bottom lip pensively.

"Look darling, don't be. I'm obliged to express the worst case scenario as with anything else in life. It's all a gamble. But trust me dear, you'll be okay. The FEDs aren't looking for people like us, they're after the thieving little estate toe-rags. You are the last dealer in town. Hahaha."

"I jolly well hope you're right about this, old man. I just hope you're right."

"Less of the old man, old girl. You'll thank me. You'll see, you'll thank me."

Watch Out Watch Me Watch You

Back home in his 'bedroom science lab', Archie packed a light rucksack with a toothbrush and deodorant, roll up tobacco, some papers and a vape. Headphones on again, over a hoodie and, of course, wearing his favourite VANS trainers, he made for a quick getaway from the house while his mother was on her mobile in the kitchen, headphones on too, pouring herself a craft gin from the brewery company she worked for.

"I'm out Mum. See ya. Don't wait up. Don't call. Text."

She came running out after him, looking trim in her house shorts and Arizona Birkenstocks.

"Arrrchieeee. Archie! Don't you dare run off..."

Slam. The door shut fast. She would never catch him.

"What am I going to do with him?" she said to herself, still in mid-conversation.

"He's running a riot of rings around me. I don't know where he goes or who he's with. He's just changed. My baby just turned into a fucking little shit. Sorry, sorry to moan, Jo. I feel so bloody helpless."

Quickly approaching 5'11, the lean-framed, green-eyed lad, strode quickly to his allegedly stolen bike, which was locked in a mate's garden nearby. His other bike was parked in the communal hallway at home. Archie had made up an elaborate lie about being mugged for his bike and subsequently was rewarded for his carelessness with another. His poor mother used to assume he wouldn't have gone far without it. Leaving his new bike at home seemed to offer some assurance of his whereabouts, he found. He did it for her own sanity as well as his.

The boy had learned how to change the tone of his voice and his eye contact with her to gain just about anything from his mother, superficially and emotionally. It wasn't just the studio equipment. A lot of the other boys at school had used the same technique. Playing the guilt card never failed. Parents always wanted to keep up with other parents in terms of generosity. They were all at it.

He jumped on his bike and rode to meet Severign in Queen's Park. The young couple sat on a bench, throwing leaves at each other playfully before rolling up some 'baccy'.

"Anyway, I asked Daddy if I could have a few friends round. Just our little group... me, you, Daisy and Bertie, Rex and Jago and he said it was okay. Can't actually believe it. Only Daisy was allowed round before."

"Hmmm? Yeah. Sounds good. There's no way anyone's meeting my nightmare mother any time soon."

"Oh, Archie...don't call her that. So, shall I start planning then?"

"Seems like you already have."

"I've been thinking."

"Yes little girl...does it hurt?"

"Ha, bloody ha. I've got this idea. Daddy's going away with his plastic Barbie soon. What if I get him and Mummy confused about the dates?"

"Ahhh, I see where you're going...jokes."

"Yeah, like they don't really talk to each other. It's 'tell ya mother this or tell your father that.'"

"They trust you, though. You could lose that."

"So. And what?"

"I dunno. They could forbid you to go out. Ground you. Blame it all on me."

"They don't even know you exist. I barely exist. It was bad enough when I was a kid. But now I have to ferry myself from pillar to post. They're a nightmare. I can do whatever I like. They've got far more important stuff to think about than me."

"No they haven't. At least you've got both parents."

"Oh Archie, not that again? Why don't you do something about it. Look again for your father. I would."

Archie grunted, while they shared the rollie.

"That's it, I've decided. I'm going to confuse the dates and we can all hang out at Daddy's. Play music, order in some pizzas, get a few beers, it's gonna be great. We could do an overnight."

"Hmmm? Yeah. Sounds dodge, but overnight would be good."

"It's a challenge, but I can make it happen. Watch me."

"Get you?" mumbled Archie, as he kissed his sweetheart.

"Mmmm, gorgeous, stop. Let's go to Bertie's place for a bit. I'll see you there. I'll walk."

"Noooooo, jump on the back."

"I'd ride my own bike if I owned one. Be careful. We don't want to get seen."

"I hate not being out in the open. It's the 21st

century, fuck's sake."

"Err, it's your mother's fault and I'm still 15. Won't be for much longer, though."

"My mum will have a fit, if I get mixed up with a girl before uni. So stop leading me on."

"Hahaha. I laugh every time you say that. Too weird babe."

"Yup. Mum is a weirdo. I'm like her surrogate boyfriend. I've stopped being her plus one. It's fucking creepy."

"Bless her beautiful baby boy. Hope I'm not like that if I have a kid." With a wide swing of his indigo denim leg, Archie took off with a peck.

"I'll race ya.", he bellowed, shooting off down the street.

*****

Bertie was the son of DJ legend Eli Stefano and stepson of Dande Lyon. He had a passion for all things house music related, just like his father. The workshop space his step mum, Dande, leased to Myrtle, housed a sound proofed annexe, a place of escape from his erratic home life, out of sight from his attention-seeking little sister, who reported his movements over his every waking hour to his parents.

He felt he had a decent crew, mostly made up of uni dropouts and skiving six formers. A mixed group of boys and girls from the typical multi-cultural backgrounds found in west London. Middle Eastern, Afro Caribbean, Polish, Spanish, Portuguese and Romany travellers.

Bertie used his boy-cave mostly at night and often crashed there in a sleeping bag between bean bags.

As a result, it stank of old fags and testosterone sweat. Rank.

One evening Severign met him while Myrtle finished off a job. His huge eyes and majestic stature made an impression on her. Then when she saw his cool friends packing themselves into the small room, one boy in particular caught her eye…Archie.

In light of the sudden invasion of teenage males, Myrtle gave Severign a pre-emptive lecture and a few stern looks about ever turning up there without her. Severign broke the rules immediately, under the pretence of looking for her mother on a few evenings she knew she wouldn't be there, perchance to catch Archie, the handsome young fellow she had spied.

Bertie had welcomed Archie into his fold after following his channel and music feeds.

Hanging out with this lot could present an opportunity to evolve into a fully fledged producer. Archie revelled in their older company. Especially knowing who Bertie's father was. He wouldn't have to go to university. Perhaps be a prodigy, grow his following to a million and get flown out to Coachella next year. His sixth form friends just seemed immature to him. These guys were the people he needed to nurture him to the top.

Eventually Archie got chatting. After a few clumsy bump-ins, orchestrated by Severign. They bonded, started WhatsApping, and quickly became inseparable. He had already bagged himself a girlfriend just by hanging out with Bertie and co. It was a sign.

At first this was where the couple hung out the most. Sometimes they were offered a draw on a toke here and there, but they were denied the harder stuff, no MDMA, no mushrooms, no coke. As the youngest two, this protective arm of the group was an unspoken code. Severign had lied about her age. She said she was 16 soon to be 17. It was a few weeks in before she fessed up to Archie who forgave her quickly, given he did not fare much better when it came to peddling the truth himself.

Holiday plans were underway for Boyd and Marisole to fly to Ibiza. Severign made a start by introducing her friends to them a week before they flew out. She decided to only ask safe bets over – Daisy, Rex and Archie – to set the right impression. They looked younger and less intimidating than the others. Had Bertie been invited it would have been straight up game over. Much older, he had that lived-in face no parent could trust, and they would not be far wrong. They only stayed for an hour or two that first visit. Enough to satisfy Boyd from jumping to conclusions about the teenagers. All well behaved and polite. He had no cause for alarm. The visit went without a hitch, much to Severign's delight, until she realised that her mother and father had been communicating more consistently than usual.

Myrtle acknowledged confirmation of Boyd's outbound and return flights. With her new business she could not afford to be unreliable. Out and about making drop offs that had to work around Severign. The idea of losing even one client and then having to tell Trotty filled her with dread. Bizarrely it was this new 'role' that brought structure to her life.

Mother and father no longer at loggerheads, Severign had no Plan B in which to play them off.

"Are you out again tonight?" she quizzed.

"Yes, but only for an hour. Just helping Liberty out with something. Don't you have homework?"

"End of term this week, remember? What's for dinner?"

"Leek and asparagus bake."

"Yum."

Severign could only smile that Liberty was involved. Whenever her mother was out with her, one hour often lapsed into the wee small hours, which meant more time with Archie. She dwelled on how much her mother had changed since the move. New and improved and yet still a little unbalanced in her opinion. In just a short time Myrtle was see-sawing from erratic to stable. She was all dressed up one moment and in loungewear the next. Her blonde, grey and ash wispy hair would alternate from glossy and well behaved to frizzy beach head. Severign processed these points of observation closely. They assisted her quest to manipulate her mother to her own ends.

Severign sneaked about when her mum was out cold, which could last up to a day and a half sometimes. The wannabe eco-warrior was not one to give in to anxiety by nature more than nurture. But there were isolated periods where she would worry. Mostly about her mother's safety, whether she would make it home alive some nights, after witnessing her drunken state on numerous occasions. Other times, it was worry about the law and her mother being imprisoned after getting caught doing drugs, the consequences of which could mean she went into care, an accute awareness since Marko-gate.

It wasn't long before Severign picked up on the changing finances at home. Her mother's cavalier attitude to expenses was a side she had not seen since she was a very little girl. Just in passing she mentioned some of her friends had a particular brand of rucksack. Next thing she knew a Kanken would appear on her bed. Another instance, involved a date with Daisy and her mother to the Hummingbird Bakery when she squeezed £30 into her hand and said: "Here, you treat them for a change."

The cabs and taxi rides exuded a categorical difference in fortune. Indeed, it was Myrtle's latest catchphrase, "just jump in a cab, darling," that continued to strike a chord. However, most noticeable was when Boyd shortchanged the child maintenance. The new response was, "no worries, make it up next time." In the past, unable to make ends meet, her mother usually went loopy when this happened. Whatever this new phase of her mother's was, life was becoming a whole lot more relaxed. Maybe it was down to the mindfulness chapbook Leafing her mother had become quietly obsessed with since a social worker recommended it during a post Marko bust-up visit. But it still didn't explain the secrecy and that eery, overall climate of murky suspicion which left Severign in fear of what further investigation might unearth.

Right Gear Right Now

The scheming plan to play her mum off against her dad, which Severign had boldly called on, left her as excited as she was overwhelmed. How could she execute her plan? Would her big night be thwarted by something unforeseeable? Then, out of the blue, the universe came to her rescue as she stared at a WhatsApp message in disbelief. Her father and his girlfriend had decided to stay in Ibiza a week longer.

[Darling we missed our flight. So staying on another week. Don't tell your Mum until Thursday — she will only make a fuss. Thanks hun, miss u x]

This was it. She was going to pack and pretend to be picked up by her Dad on the original date. The junior sit-up was set up.

*****

"Mummy. Dad's here. I'm going down."
"Wait darling, do you need any money? Say hi for me."
"Thank you. Text you later."
Myrtle yelped at the joy of freedom. That all elusive child free time. Time she had to use as wisely (or unwisely) as she pleased. The flat to herself, she locked the door of the study, approached the shelf to undertake the tedious weigh and wrap chore. A

new problem had emerged having barely started. Some clients were stating a preference for their gear in paper rather than the tiny self-seal polythene bags which prone to condensation made the powder cloggy. Sometimes she did the bagging under the light of the angle-poise lamp or when she was tired, sat at the desk and worked under the marble base green banker's lamp.

Naturally, as an artist her fingers were adept at this fiddly part of the job, but it was monotonous. She had to be methodical in her approach as opposed to her usual flappable self. An awkward characteristic she used to laugh off. It was as if this new trade had spawned a whole new skill set. It honed her arithmetic and perfected her forward planning that focused her mindset which in turn fed positively into other areas of her life.

Her time was less haphazard. Gone were the days when she tripped over her own feet to catch up with herself. Only the fatigue that came with poor sleeping patterns and come downs were the only unavoidable blot on an otherwise unblemished landscape.

*****

There was no knowing the source of Severign's cunning. Her first love, Archie, undoubtedly precipitated her grand scheming. Her disregard for the child/parent bond came as a result of this last house move. Two more years at least before she could leave for university and get as far away from their lack of control as possible. Any uni in Scotland appealed to her. She dreamed of being completely out of reach, even from her extended family in Winchester and Dorset. They adored her, but she still felt claustrophobic under the family gaze.

There was no turning back now. The WhatsApp group invitation had gone out. Severign was armed with more cash than she usually ever had. She went out and shopped for mega pack crisps and snacks, chocolates and pasta salads, making sure she had Fair Trade, organic and gluten free options where possible. She also loaded up on oven ready pizzas, water and 'full fat Coke'. Archie joined her and helped carry the supplies to her father's place.

Bertie, Rex and Jago were providing the beers. Daisy was going to raid her mother's drinks cupboard, who thought she was having a sleepover at another friend's house covering for her.

Severign found it nerve-wracking having her pals round. The strange liberation overlapped by fear was intoxicating. Everyone arrived almost at once. She got the keys to the patio doors where they sat on metal chairs by the dormant BBQ. It was such a grown up setting, with the solar lights and ashtrays already in place. The downstairs toilet by the kitchen meant none of her guests had any reason to snoop around her Daddy's home, leaving less clues of visitors.

Daisy arrived first. You could sense the anticipation in the air.

"Do I look alright, Sev?" asked Daisy, pulling down her Berksha cropped top. "I couldn't make more of an effort or my mum would've got suspicious. She never misses a trick."

"You look fine, silly, like always. So glad you're doing this with me."

"I've got your back. Sick, isn't it?"

"Don't, I can't even…"

"Are you nervous?".

"Yeah. I am dead meat if they find out."

"If you are, so am I. Fuck it, shit's happening now."

Then, oh so les affaire, in their Supreme branded leisurewear sweatpants and Nike Air Max trainers, the girls about turned and started preparing for the session.

The boys arrived…

Despite a cacophony of faux street dialect inflections blended with the Queen's English, as the young people spoke over each other there was a clear comprehension of everything said.

"This is alright, Severign."

She nodded emphatically, then caught herself, and tried to play it down.

"Yes, girl. Nice set up. We got booze, some smoke and other bits and pieces…yeah, this is nice."

"We need some music, though, innit?" chimed Archie. His mini speaker had a heavy bass as he played his latest mix from his phone.

"So what's in that likkle house, Sev?" asked Jago.

"Ah, the outhouse? Daddy calls it The Den. Original, duh." she responds sarcastically.

"Shed, den, hideaway. No disrespect, man is up to su'ton up there…hahaha."

"I know he is. I caught him and his mate burning. They had this giant bag of weed too."

"Yeah, right. Bare jokes, fam," laughed Jago.

"No, seriously. He doesn't know that I know. As a matter of fact, I've known about his shit since I was in Year 2! But I never say anything. He just yells when he sees me walking up there, especially when his mate's around."

The group could all relate and fell about laughing. They were getting louder as they interjected with their own similar stories.

"My Dad has a patch in my uncle's greenhouse. He grows prize orchids, so we're not allowed near it, but there's some other things blossoming, if you know what I mean."

"My mum buys it from the Avon lady, but I promise you, I haven't yet seen one beauty product in my life. Just the paper bag."

And so it went on until Bertie interjected. "You have the keys, Severign?"

She couldn't lie. She knew where they were.

"Yes, of course."

"Let's go and rest there. Will be less noise. Don't want to bring attention to the neighbours.

We can get next level chill."

"Makes sense," agreed Rex.

Severign was cornered.

"Yeah, no worries, guys. Grab a few bits while I go and get the keys."

Archie followed after her into the kitchen.

"Are you sure about this, Sev? Don't feel under pressure. I can steer it so we go back to Bertie's."

"No... No. I'm good with it. Bertie's right. Not gonna poo poo my first sesh."

"Sesh? Sesh? Get you."

"Don't take the piss...I come from a long line of pedigree druggies, don't forget."

Giddy with rebellion, the pair snogged briefly, then she demanded he looked away as she scooped the key from the drawer underside.

'The Den' was a fantastic guest space, carpeted with a kitchenette and shower room. A sofa bed and bean bag around a coffee table and TV. Just the stench of stale weed and tobacco tarnished its allure.

But Severign still needed to get something off her chest, and plucked up the courage to address the group.

"Guys, please no selfies or 'gramming or anything

while you're here."

"This is a down-low ting, we get it, sis," smirked Jago, shoving his phone back into his pocket.

"Yes," announced Bertie. "This is an undercover takeover."

Severign was enthralled by his approval. They all were. Daisy found four shot glasses in the kitchenette. "Here, guys, we'll have to share, only a handful of glasses. Let's do shots. Tequila or Sambuca? Who wants what?"

Archie took his cue under the current of excitement and whacked his speaker on blast. The little crew were 'lit'.

The gear was being prepped in earnest. Cross-legged, the young couple looked on as usual, Severign trying to conceal her unease.

"I think I'll just ice for the drinks," she blurted.

"Nah, we're good. Chill."

Archie looked at her embarrassed. Her embarrassment was making him embarrassed. This awkwardness hadn't occurred before. There was something about being in 'The Den'.

The forbidden 'Den', quite a change from Bertie's annexe.

"Here, do you want to try some? Just a small bit, take the edge off. You seem edgy."

"Er, I dunno."

Inside Severign was panicking.

"I will," volunteered Archie.

"Ah, about time, Archie, man. Wondered when you was going to step up."

"Yeah. Well, I'm here now."

"Me too Bertie. I'm good for a bit. A small one," said Severign.

Daisy grimaced at her mate, ever so slowly shaking her head in a warning of disapproval. Bertie chopped up the lines of coke like raised soil in an allotment. He pointed his family debit card, counting the heads getting involved.

"Daisy? You in?"

"Yeah," she exclaimed, immediately catching herself off guard.

She could not allow herself as the host to be left out. As the boys attempted to go first, Severign chucked a smug glance. It said, no turning back now. We will remember this time.

Bertie turned one of Boyd's DVD jewel cases away from Rex. "Manners Rex. Ladies first."

In trepidation, Severign kneeled over, took the £10 note, rolled it just like she had seen her mother do illicitly, thousands of times before, through a doorway, and whiffed the powder up in one swift suction.

"Jeez," chuckled Bertie.

They all joined in.

This threw Daisy off for a brief moment.

"Come on then, Dais...," urged Severign, challenging her friend to do better.

In another swift movement, Daisy had done her first line, followed by a delicate cough identical to her bestie.

This wasn't actually Archie's first time, but he had never done it in front of Severign. He wasn't really a fan of it.

As the plastic square went round, the banter got louder more pronounced as the inner buzz of the collective played out. After Bertie did his line, he spotted the light switch and turned it off. Only the solar lights crept through the small window, cradling them in a campfire like atmosphere.

Bertie started the chat.

"So how do you like where you live now, Severign? Westbourne Grove sides I hear?"

"Yes. It's lovely thanks."

"You're moving up in the world, aren't you?"

"She's got a study in her flat." said Archie, digging her out some more.

"Hey, you haven't even been inside."

The two flew into a finger fight, only curbed it when they felt stared at, like two kids mucking about. They tried to gather themselves to continue the talk.

"He's always doing that. Stop. I'm glad we moved. Hated that other place. I hated the place before that, come to think of it."

"Sounds like your people are on the run. My folks are like that," butted in Jago.

"At least your mum's not shacking up with every guy she meets. I dread it every time mine brings another guy back."

"Sounds like your mum has a lot of friends, Sev."

"What I mean is, I've lived in someone else's house. Never felt like mine – ours. Like here, at my Dad's feels more like home."

"Yeah I feel the same at my Dad's too," said Rex, adding, "I got a dog, my own room, TV and games. Nobody is allowed in my room neither. It's good. It's miles away, though."

"I just want to get my own place," moaned Bertie. "I'm almost sleeping in that workshop full time, bruv. My Dad, he's cool, but my step-mum is bare problems. She is nice to me, to please my Dad. She acts like she cares, but she don't, and she hates me because I can see through her act. My Dad's a fool."

"My mum said she brought you up," Severign intervened. "What happened to your real mum...erm.

Sorry is it okay to ask?"

"Yeah...she's got mental health issues and stuff...so..." Bertie tailed off.

"Haven't they all though," reasoned Archie. "My mother sounds like your step- mother. She's always on me. I get no peace. All I hear is Archie. Archie. Arrrchieeee! Have you done this, have you done that? Don't go here, stay over there. Always asking me, why I like something. Why do I have to explain my existence to her?"

"I think most mothers are like this. Especially when you get older. It's like they can't stand losing the power over us. Like, we're not children anymore?" said Daisy, never one to miss a debate, and talking more freely than ever after her first line. She continued.

"My mum, she loves her drink. She thinks I don't know. But she got a problem and my Dad just puts up with it. She's awful to him. It's horrible."

"Won't she miss these?" A beaming Jago held up the tequila and Sambuca bottles. "Give us a shot, then."

*****

Pleasure-seeking hedonist to her heart, Myrtle had seized on the offer of a triple A VIP wristband to the Passcode Festival - her first big outdoor engagement with Trotty out of the picture. There was a bit of extra prep to do, but it was all part of the business model. The line-up was exclusive, backstage was going to be about establishing herself as Trotty's hands, which would stand her in good stead ongoing.

The drive to Cambridgeshire was long enough, but for all the fun of the festival, on arrival the arduous logistical nightmares really began with the hunt for car parks or base camps. Depending on the organisers, collecting wristbands or buying tokens created its own set of problems...everlasting queues, losing things or getting lost yourself. But just like a mother giving birth, keen festival goers are good at collective amnesia, and readily return to repeat the manic merry-go-round over and again the following year. Myrtle in a light waxed camo-jacket and denim shorts, hair in pigtails was all set for where the adventure would lead her. Passcode Festival was relatively new, promoted by established music event promoters she trusted. She welcomed all that it entailed...the challenge, as always, to sustain her buzz no matter the hazards that came with it. She had seen and done it all. This time was going to be very different. Serving up on such a large scale while keeping her wits about her was would be a big test. AAA (Access All Areas) meant that the crew she was with could drive into the easily located VIP car park without intrusive searches.

There was a quiet calm to be found backstage. With sound systems audience-facing, it was possible to have an orderly conversation without shouting. Usually spacious Portaloo-free zones with arty seating areas sponsored by leading drinks firms. Complimentary cocktail in hand, Myrtle found this to be one of the nicer perks of going VIP. It wasn't just about milling with the artistes. Smart winnebagos for bathrooms with branded liquid soap and hot water was a civilised addition. Even then, she was someone happy to wear the same clothes over a three-day weekender.

She made the most of the daylight hours to remember faces, outfits and basically recall who she would be supplying, as discussed prior to her arrival. Plus also remember to send word to any other faces who had decided to come last minute. Clients also had a habit of dropping out last minute, too. Nothing was on tick. Pay up on receipt, right gear, right now. Those were strict rules to adhere Trotty laid out for festivals. The other order was not to get high on your own supply until everything was sold. This was a mission Myrtle was determined to be accomplish. She hadn't come to miss out on the fun either

She prepared her stock answer for the people she knew outside of her regulars.

"I've got a few bits…mudma and coke…but running low on account of the demand here. I can put one aside for later just in case, but you know how it is. When it's gone. In fact, I don't know where I'll be, or whether I'm staying for the whole weekend yet. It depends really…"

Her mantra was, 'when the drugs run out, the fun stops, but don't stop until you get enough'. How much is enough no one ever knows, but panic buying is a thing. Myrtle knew how to trigger those doubts. Firstly, she had to ensure three clients got their orders. One was a sound engineer, a music PR manager and one member of the Passcode production team.

The light show kicked in and the festival came alive, the music seemed louder and

the much-underrated sound of the generators, never far away from good times, powered along.

*****

Bertie rapidly chopped up another set of lines. Five nice neat rows. There were no questions or expectations this time. They sniffed, chuckled or coughed. Then the chat took off again.

"You know, my step-mother Dande, she goes to AA. I don't really know why. Again, they hide this stuff away from me. They're so secretive. I know she goes AA. I wish she would just drink without the guilt. Her temper, man...it's...it's...I can't even say how bad it is. She talks to my Dad like shit. Worse since they got married."

"At least Dande is going AA. My mum..." said Severign "...she's a total wino. I swear she knocks back so much wine, it's a joke. She looks different, she sounds weird and she pretends she was only 'jolly'...fuck's sake. She's a fucking drunk."

"My mum's an 'alchy' as well. She's working for a craft gin company of all things and I reckon she drinks more than she sells," joked Archie. "Her and her mate, every two weeks, they get hammered. I mean properly smashed. Toppling over. Wetting themselves. They always end up slagging men off and the way my mum slates my gran... well..."

"My mum slags off both my grans," added Rex, dumping his shit into the mix. "She hates my teachers. She hates her friends. She hates her boss. She hates my dad, of course."

"Why are they so moany?" asked Jago.

"Issues, man. Issues all over the shop," replied Archie. "I don't even know who my Dad is. She gets herself into a stink anytime I ask. I have a right to know. Once my gran was trying to tell me and they kicked off. One time she made my gran cry right in front of me. It was horrible. She's a heartless bitch, my mum. All about her. How she wants things."

"Fucking hell, Archie."

"You got to find out who he is...where he is."

"You have a right to know..."

The group rallied round their pal.

"It's alright. I don't ask nothing anymore, "said a resigned Archie. I barely speak to her, as it goes. Just a means to an end."

"You should track your father down. How hard can it be? Bet he's on social media. Do you know his name? I'll help you find him," offered Rex.

"Mate. I know my way around tech. I would've tracked him by now if the bitch would even tell me his name."

"Easy mate. We got you bruv," said a calm Jago, rolling their next joint.

Severign sneaked a consoling palm over Archie's lower back.

"I can't understand what the deal is. It's so frustrating when she shuts down on me." They all nodded in agreement.

"Don't give up Arch, keep strong," said Bertie, reassuringly. "I went looking for information on my mother because they wouldn't tell me nuffink. Didn't like what I found. But the pressure I was feeling eased up. I was gonna blow, you know."

"I have a friend who can hack anything. Check me. He can get any information out there. Trus'."

"Might follow you up on that."

"Whenever you're ready, star," assured Jago.

"When will they learn that all the secrecy is more harmful in the end?" Rex was hoping his philosophical question would take the conversation in another direction.

"I know, for instance," said Severign. "...that my Daddy's stash of weed is inside the multipack of kitchen towels under the sink over there. He thinks I'm stupid."

"Aight," came the ensemble in unison at the disclosure. Loving the attention, Severign dived over to demonstrate the facts. She pulled out a large freezer food bag of weed like a rabbit from a hat. "See. Told ya."

"Bet that's some good shit."

"Let's have a little go on some of that..."

"I'll take a little bit out. It's strong. I tried a bit before."

Daisy raised an eyebrow, sure that Severign was lying.

Jago took the extraction from Severign as if it was a green baby sparrow fallen from a tree. Then she carefully placed the puff back as she found it.

"Severign," demanded Daisy. "Let's get some ice."

"Anybody want anything from the house?"

"Think we brought everything in..."

Daisy grabbed her mate by the elbow as they marched down the garden path amid a flurry of argumentative whispers.

"Sev, what're you doing, giving out your dad's stuff like that? Stop showing off. We are in so much trouble if we get caught. What time is it? I've got to text my mum. You should too."

"Shit. Forgot about that. Better do it now. Even if it's late."

The girls leaned on the breakfast bar and sealed their fate for the evening texting monumental lies to their parents.

As they approached The Den they could hear boyish testosterone guffaws. Whatever mysogynistic banter had them physically rolling on their backs ceased abruptly as the girls entered.

"What's the craic, guys?" Daisy tilted her head maternally.

"Nuffink."

"Nuffink? Grow up you lot."

The early hours of the night saw them settle in to yet more lines.

"Severign. Thank you for this."

"You're welcome. I'm dead meat if my parents get wind of this."

"Thought you said it was alright?"

"Yeah it is. Just like, I'm working on a few things. Let's forget about that. Guess what? I think I can tell you guys, we're like family right?"

"Oh jeez, Sev," shuddered Daisy.

"You're so funny tonight, Sev. Spill." Bertie egged her on.

"Whisper it to me first...," begged Archie.

"No, it's just going back to what we were talking about before. Y'know secrets and lies 'n shit."

"Oooh, it's all coming out now..." laughed Rex.

"Stop interrupting. Tell you what. Let's play truth or dare."

"Game...bringing game? Really? Just speak girl," pushed Jago.

"Truth or dare?" insisted Severign.

"Truth, duh." Archie rolled his eyes.

"Well...my mum...she...my mum...she. She does coke. Lots of it."

The gang fell about laughing, cackling it was all too much.

"What? What have I said?"

"You said nothing, you nutter."

"Will someone tell me. I don't get it?"

"I think..." Jago intervened, "...I think...we can safely say that all our parents take gear. And lots of it. Hahaha."

"Oh, I get it now, they're all on it?"

"Told you to run it by me first," nudged Archie.

Indignant, Severign decided to step things up a gear.

"Okay, then. What if I was to tell you she was serving up?"

"What? Your mum's a dealer?" Archie was taken aback, really wishing Severign had checked with him on this one.

"Hmmm. Got your attention now, have I? She's always done it, I think. For a long time, she just wasn't making any money, not like she does now anyway. I thought she only did enough to feed her own habit."

"Get you?" said Bertie, not convinced. "How do you know? She could just be buying and using."

"No. If she was, she's not doing that anymore. She's upped her game because all of a sudden we are in this posh flat, she gets me cabs everywhere to save her time. She's also been buying me loadsa stuff, which is just a waste, cluttering up the planet like some mindless consumer."

"Huh, huh, sounds good to me."

"I don't want to be another consumer, thanks. She can keep it. The main thing is I know, but she doesn't know that I know."

"Have you told your dad?" wondered Daisy.

"I am not a complete idiot, Daisy. That would be catastrophic."

"You seem pretty calm about it, considering."

"What else is there? Am I supposed to say, dear Mummy can you stop dealing now? I don't want to visit you in prison."

"Whoa..." There was a gasp. She continued.

"I know what she is up to, especially with certain friends of hers. What gets to me is the whole charade of whispers and sneaking around trying to act normal, whenever I walk into a room."

A calm disquiet engulfed the group. All that could be heard was the heart thumping bass of Archie's tunes.

Bertie broke the pause.

"Do you know what you're saying, Sev?"

Archie felt entitled to repeat the question. "Is your mum really serving up?"

The naive 15-year-old nodded profusely, basking in the release her confession brought. She had never shared this information before. She had been weighed down with it, unsure how to deal with it. Unable to talk to them. The burden of secrecy was all she had known all her life. She existed in a fear of what might happen to her mother one day for a long time. This was it. She was ready to hang on to every word her cohorts had to say about it.

"Wow…"

Rex looked up at Bertie then added: "Thought it was just me. My parents are involved as well."

Severign shuffled herself enthusiastically towards Rex. "Do you know how they get it or where they hide it?"

"I don't know who they get it from. But what I do know is that sometimes my mum drops my dad off outside this house that we never go in. We wait and then he comes back with a magazine or during Christmas, a greeting card…or at Easter, chocolate eggs, but usually some sort of design magazine. What's weird, is that he never reads magazines at home. I didn't think anything of it for years until one time my little sister banged her head on the kitchen work top. She was screaming and bleeding so much, everyone was panicking around the house getting plasters and mopping her face with kitchen towels.

They took her to the upstairs bathroom to clean her up. Man, she was milking it. I needed the toilet myself so I went and used my parents ensuite. I saw an open magazine on the floor with some pages ripped out in squares. I didn't realise what they were for really. I used the toilet, washed my hands and when I looked at the ledge on the side, I saw these small bags of white chalk balls, man. I kind of knew, but at the same time I didn't? So I legged it outta there quick because their bathroom was out of bounds. Suddenly it all made sense."

"Did they catch you?" asked Severign.

"Well, my mum was cleaning up the blood from the floor with the towel and my Dad looked over at me through the door. I think he had an idea, but didn't want to make an issue of it. I was about 11, I think then. As I started to get older I was hoping he would be straight with me. I'm 19 now and still he won't man up. Those little eight balls are the only balls he's got. I have zero respect for him."

"Fucking hell, Rex..." Severign went in. "It's cray! Do you feel yourself creeping about, scared to catch them all the time? I do."

"I felt weird. Like my house just changed. Every time I opened a cupboard or went in the fridge, I kept thinking I might find something."

"Me too. I hated when my mother asked me to fetch something, in case I accidentally found her stuff. I won't go in her bag or coat pockets. If she wants something she has to get it herself. I just can't do it."

"Once I knew what was happening," added Rex. "I started hating when they had friends round, especially on a school night. We were either in bed early or going to stay with the grandparents. But before we left, I could tell they was glad to see the back of us."

Bertie's down turned bottom lip seemed frozen into shape, as he slowly nodded. "So, they was selling as well?"

"That was before they divorced, anyway. We had rolls of cash in the family safe," continued Rex. "Lots of it. We also had people coming over for like 5 or 10 minutes at a time. It was worse over Bank Holidays, I remember that."

"I know, between term times the pattern changed from one holiday to the next," said Severign. "It was mostly other mums. She told me they were in a parenting group. That was the old days. She can be gone for a weekend or whole nights at a time now. I don't know if it's because I'm older she feels she can sell more?"

"Guys. This shit is real. I suggest what's said or heard doesn't leave here," stressed Bertie. "Folks gotta do what they gotta do. My Dad, because of his DJing work, it's an open secret what they get up to in their world. We used to catch them out on holidays in Ibiza all the time. It's no biggie. It's just life."

"But what else are they lying about though?" piped up Archie.

"Your mum definitely does coke," said Severign.

"Yeah, not loads though. It's a party thing. She and her friends used to rave, but not anymore. She's just thirsty."

"Like my mum," muscled in Daisy.

"My mum is sneaky in other ways," whispered Archie.

"Like?"

"Like, she won't tell me who my father is," continued Archie, returning to the paternal theme that haunted him. "Nobody will tell me. I feel like a dirty secret. I ain't gonna lie, I bare betrayal."

"A man needs to know his father, I don't care what anyone says," cried out Jago.

"All I've got is that he didn't want me. It was for my own good. She ain't telling me... and that's that. But I'm gonna find him, though. Somebody knows."

"I'll help you Archie. We can do it over the summer," said Severign.

"Thought we was playing truth or dare?" reminded Daisy, refilling the drinks.

"Turn this one up, Archie. Love this one," enthused Bertie. "Let's rack up another one of these."

That marked the end of truth or dare. The time flew by and the blue light of dawn flashed through the cracks of the black out blinds. Some of them had dozed off a bit. But the energy was still there for the hardcore present. Jago, Bertie, Archie and Severign quietly voiced their cynical and humorous take on the world. That was until Jago checked his phone. The conversation took another direction.

"Nah. Nah. Not Mensah. Not him...," he blubbed.

"What's happened, J?"

He couldn't reply to Severign for wiping his tear-filled eyes with his denim shirt sleeve. His phone languished in his other outstretched palm.

"Aw mate, what's happened?" He shook his head in disbelief. In shock.

"We've lost him. They took him. It's so senseless. I can't even...," he sobbed.

"Who? Who Jago?"

"My friend's boy. Stabbed. He's 13. He was 13..."

Severign held Jago, while he cried, Archie joined in, then Bertie.

The solemn commotion alarmed Daisy and Rex from their snooze.

"What's happened?" they asked, concerned.

"Do you need to shoot off now?"

"A friend of Jago's been stabbed."

"Oh my God, Jago. I'm so sorry. Is he alright?"

"He's dead. He's dead! Thirteen and dead...man, these youngers, it's too soon, the struggle..."

"Jesus Christ. What the fuck is wrong with people?" said Rex.

"No. I ain't going anywhere. I'll get stopped. Is it okay to stay on a bit?"

"Of course. Can I make you a drink, a coffee or something?"

"Nah. I'm alright...thanks."

"Ok, hun, I'll get you some water anyway."

"I can't imagine what it must be like. A boy that used to go to my school...he got stabbed. So sad."

"Same, I know of two people who died couple years now," added Bertie. "Bare madness. I know how you feel, bro."

"It makes you think, doesn't it?" added Daisy.

Jago raised his chin, stroked his neck, staving off his frustration for what he assumed was going to be a verbal attack about his loss.

"Leave it Daisy." Archie read the sensitivity of the situation.

"No. It's alright. Think what?" Jago was on the edge of an outburst.

"Well, we are all sitting here getting on it. We don't think about killing each other to get it, do we? How do they..."

"Hang on...you're jumping to conclusions there...how do we know it's drug related...gang related, even?" suggested Rex.

"They, as you put it, aren't exactly using. They're part of the chain in supplying the stuff. They're on the hustle. Trying to make a likkle change. They've got nuffink," blasted Jago.

"Okay, guys, let's bring this down a notch," interjected Bertie. "Do you wanna talk about it, J? Daisy's just trying to make sense of it. We all are. But if now is not the time?"

"I ain't going nowhere. Yeah. Let's talk about it."

"Don't get angry though, we're on your side hun," said Severign

"I'm lucky. Kind of. I live in a nice house away from the estates. But I still have connections struggling out there. We got out. But what I can tell you is that little Mensah was a good kid. His mum works hard. Thing is she works shifts in the NHS, so he's home alone all the time. His Dad, he's my brother's mate, that's how I know them. He lives somewhere else. But he works in security and isn't around most nights. Even I've been roped in sometimes to go sit with him. It's like we knew he shouldn't be left alone, but he was so sensible for his age. Oh God. I still can't believe it. The little man."

"Did he get mixed up with some bad kids then?"

"I don't know, I'm sure they didn't see it coming. This will break his dad."

"You hear about it, don't you? They spot the 'home alones' and groom them for gangs."

"Why didn't he tell anyone? Could he not tell someone?" Severign pleaded.

"Like you, you mean? You didn't tell anyone about your mum dealing, did you? Not 'til tonight."

Everyone frowned at Jago for this jibe.

"Yes. You're right. I don't know what made me even tell you either."

"Secrets and fucking lies," scolded Archie.

"If the gangs got to him and he didn't pick a side they would kill him anyway. Either way he didn't stand a chance. I don't know what he knew, what he did or with who. I just got this text. He's dead."

Jago took some deep breaths.

"I don't get why they have to murder a young person, though," said Rex. "I can understand criminals fighting among themselves, but this is crazy!"

"Rex, that's the cowardly part of it. Some Mr Big, Mrs Big, King pin, call them whatever, they must be setting them up. The kids aren't old enough or clever enough to strategise. No way."

"Strategise? You make it sound like some corporate operation."

"Well it has to be, doesn't it? Do the sums, man," said Jago. "Listen, think about it. Every city in this country...Leeds, Manchester, Birmingham, Nottingham, Essex...not even saying London. My mum was getting a start-up business, selling sauces on the side. If she wanted to make more and sell it to every town and city, she needs a distributor. It's like, not that easy to sell anything without that. It's well complicated. The people who want to help want a massive cut for helping her supply the sauce. It's no joke. She was going to be tied up in a deal for years. What I'm saying is someone is shipping the gear in. Like masses of it so that the whole country can be supplied. Count it. That is a lot of coke to go round when you really actually start counting it. The chain of marketing, supply and demand, which we're covering in my A Level Business Studies, is not to be underestimated. I'm pretty sure that no 13-year-old kid has studied it. I'm also sure most of them haven't even left their area, let alone been on a plane. It's bigger than the streets. The whole set up works like a well-oiled machine, even slicker than Amazon. Order and it gets delivered day or night. Anytime, anywhere. The drug business model has been perfected. And my mate's kid is a victim of it. You may not agree, but that's how I see it."

"Never thought about it like that," said Severign.

"Nor me," reasoned Rex. "What I wanna know is...is there like a coke mountain or something? Is there so much out there that increases the competition? The violence, the knifing thing? Seems so unnecessary. Is someone putting them up to that?"

"How the hell would I know, Rex? I'm just saying, in terms of business studies and watching my mum's sauce business, I'm not saying anythin' new, it's all on Netflix anyway."

"Think Jay Z learned the business of business in the game. The trick is to get out quick and clean up your act. Kids killing kids ain't the way."

"Don't bring Jay Z into this. Your parents are dealing. They're privileged and educated so what's their excuse?"

"Oh Jago," said Daisy. "That's a bit harsh, hun. It's different for them. They're just selling among their friends, no gangs involved."

"Yeah, my Dad's lot can barely make a fist when they've been on it, let alone hold a knife."

"Ask yourselves. What's so different about what your parents do, though?" Jago was understandably uptight in his grief. "They're free to make poor choices. See if I was to leave here now, there's more of a likelihood of me getting stopped and searched by the Feds. Why? Because my dark skin identifies me as gangster before I've even opened my mouth. Doesn't matter that my mum's got a cool job, that I live in a nice house. I don't get to be a student experimenting with recreationals. Your middle-class parents get to do as they please..."

"Your parents are middle-class too, Jago."

"I know...but until my mother speaks, she stereo-typed as a single parent bringing up a hustler."

"Whatever you say, the stabbings. It's black boys killing other black boys."

"Hey guys...this is getting heavy," pointed out Bertie.

"It's real, bro. My friend's kid, man. Tch. If it was a white kid hanging out with his neighbours who are white, suddenly it's just 'a stabbing'. Black boys hang out with other black boys, the way I see it, is teenager stabbing teenager. Colour don't come into it."

"My dad says it's liberalism gone wrong."

"It's more than that. If you think about it," argued Bertie. "The death toll of young black males adds up to the amount of young people suffering from mental health disorders, such as Bulimia and Anorexia, and let's not forget self-harming," he added, sounding very informed on the subject matter.

"Hmmm? Someone at school died of anorexia."

"My friend's cousin committed suicide after self-harming. She hid it from everyone."

"This is depressing. If young people aren't killing each other they're killing themselves. Bare madness. Fuck."

"What about cyber bullying. I know someone who, well...it's just horrible."

"I was cyber-bullied. It fucked me up. I'm out the other side, now, but still...," reflected Bertie.

"See what I mean? Young people dying at home, don't count as gangsta. But to my mind it's just as bad as the stabbings, if it ends someone's life."

"Young people just dying everywhere man."

"Why do you think this is happening?" Daisy quizzed further.

"Someone needs to find a way to break the cycle."

"I hear that…"

They collectively nodded in agreement, in a brief moment of sad reflection.

"Sorry about your friend Jago."

*****

By 4am Myrtle had put away her portfolio and, escorted by her designated driver, had locked it safely in the 4x4. She was disappointed that she ended up with a mere two grams for her personal use. It was day one and she had already sold out. How amateur, she scolded herself, frustrated at miscalculating the demand. These revellers were sitting targets, the perfect seller's market. There was so much more she could have sold. The crew she was with was surprised as well. 'Schoolgirl error, Myrtle', rang through her mind. But in reality this, she reassured herself, was not how the game worked. It wasn't an exact science. She focused on the positives, unlike the car boot sales, which she had a penchant for, where she would leave with more goods than she sold.

She rejoined her crew, greeted with hugs and kisses like a long-lost family member, swallowed a bump of 'mud' and got on it with them at the side of the stage, the DJ blasting festival anthems to rev up the battered crowds. The Frankie Knuckles remix of Blind by Hercules & Love Affair provided a real moment. Some gifted her a pill for later or a bump as a thank you from a previous session. She began to think her jacket pocket had more gear in than she had sold before she got there. Happy days! Let the fun and games begin. Time to celebrate selling out, not bemoan not selling enough. At least she could relax now.

Peeble Excuse

As midday approached Daisy and Severign cooked up a storm. The pasta had all been devoured, so the girls improvised. The smell of eggs and reheated leftover pizza woke the boys from their deep snoring slumber. The strong weed smoked had counteracted the pokey coke they had been snorting.

Fed and watered, the boys dispersed hoodies up, except for Archie who stayed back to help the girls with the big clean up. Ashtrays, glasses, pizza boxes and empties were washed, put away and binned. They were satisfied to leave The Den gleaming better than the condition they found it and the house kitchen was spotless.

Severign ran a last exacting eye over the surfaces and hidden corners, the consequences of failure was not an option. She and her team high-fived their efforts.

After waving them off, Severign surrendered to the anti-climax of her big night.

A nagging headache subsided as she took herself off to bed with a glass of water. She had been so absorbed with organising her evening she had almost overlooked the big lie she had yet to uphold. Everything over the next few days would depend on her Dad staying out of radio contact with her mother. This was a job for WhatsApp and she would have to stay connected by playing the dutiful daughter role she knew so well. Asking them for advice on clothes, all things education related and the emotional trips down memory lane. She knew they lived for reassurances of the good times and how happy she had been and still is. Myrtle and Boyd lapped these nuggets up wholesale. These simple texts, little and often stopped her parents checking up on each other. She was the bargaining chip between them, it was not tech science.

She had never been home alone for this many days consecutively before. She flicked through Spotify, mainly listening to Bedroom by Litany on repeat. The next 72 hours would be critical.

*****

Whilst her daughter seemed to be in buoyant mood, Myrtle had made the most of her bonus 'child-free-time'.

But Day Three at the festival was a wash out. Myrtle and the crew could barely walk to the 4x4. They slept in until the driver felt ready to hit the road.

Myrtle was a mess. Just about coping. Blocked sinuses, a runny nose, a hoarse voice, all usual post-festival symptoms, but she now also walked with a severe limp after falling onto a table.

Three days was more than enough. She could not remember if she had eaten any of that amazing street food. Perhaps she did catch the headline act after all...while, the jury was out on snogging some random fella in a poncho. Her cross-body saddle bag held her wallet. The money had better be in there. She could not afford to check in front of everyone in the vehicle, or even at the service station. This would have to wait until she got home.

Paranoid on the come down, in a semi-comatose state, she dreamt the money had gone. She woke up, clutched her bag. Dreamt the money had gone. Repeat. It hadn't. And thankfully, as arranged, she was the first drop off once they returned to London.

*****

As the week played out Severign successfully navigated in and around a series of lies via phone and text. She came away feeling like a young adult, and independent of mind after hearing her peer's perspective on family life during the sit up. She developed an acceptance of her situation. She wasn't going to play the victim of circumstance for anyone. As soon as she was at uni she would have less and less to do with her parents and create her own more honest world. She reasoned that she was temporarily driven to be dishonest because her parents were dishonest with her. She pledged defiance against their double standards. She felt loved, but not without that thin veil of underlying obligation. The more she played Boyd and Myrtle off each other, the easier it got to manipulate their egos to suit her own ends.

Sitting under a tree by their park, Severign and Archie, besotted with each other, twisting each other's hair, creating loved up selfies via various phone apps. They lolled and rolled about without a care, laughing at the weird and wonderful people passing by. Standard west London eccentric characters.

"Oh no, Arch...just got a text. Daddy's back."

"Fuck, hahaha. We tidied up, okay? Don't worry it'll be fine."

"No. No," said Severign, reading on. "He says 'we need to talk young lady, come over right now before I call your mother.' Fuck."

"Shit, we missed something. You're in big trouble. Don't drag my name into it. I'm in enough bother."

"Fuck you. Thanks for the back up," she said, thumping Archie in his side.

"Hey, don't make this my fault. You'd better go and sort it out. Do you know what you're going to say?"

"Depends what it is. Shit. Shit. Shit."

"Do you want me to come with you? What's he gonna do?"

"Oh, he won't hit me or anything. He'll yell and try to be serious and then it will blow over. It's Mummy, though. I hate when they're both on side, against me."

"You better get going, then."

"I'd better face him on my own. Hopefully, Barbie doll will be there to soften things...text you after. If you don't hear from me, Mummy's buried me in the basement."

"Seriously, if it gets on top, call me."

Archie's concern, albeit brief, was enough to strengthen her resolve...to stand up for herself. She was not a child now.

On her way to her father's, Severign got a call from her agitated and confused mother, wondering why she was being summoned for a chat with him. The great twisted lies about Boyd's return from Ibiza unravelled at speed.

Severign's abrupt response was, "I can't talk now. Stop yelling. I will call after Daddy does his share of yelling at me too."

Then she rang off.

As Severign strolled up to the path of her Willesden second home, anxiety crept in. The door was open, Marisole just leaving for the cab outside. She was extremely tanned and barely dressed as usual, busting out of her outfit.

"Hi darling. I've left something for you in the kitchen. It's a gorgeous bikini you'll love it. Come here, mwaw.", she purred, stooping to air kiss Severign's cheeks.

"Get in here!" shouted Boyd from the lowest register of his lungs.

A relieved Marisole, giving a half-hearted wave, glanced back for a split second. Severign, sullenly shuffling into the kitchen, for once, wished her 'step-mum-in-waiting' had stayed, to help dilute the situation.

Boyd grabbed his daughter's wrist and led her around the bins.

"Dad you can't treat me like this. Let go of me and I'll talk to you properly."

First the kitchen bin, then he walked her to the outside bins, The Den and its kitchenette bin and finally the shower room bin.

"What's this?" he yelled at each point.

"You can't do this, stop," she demanded.

"Can't I? Can't I? You just go in there, sit down and tell me who's been round here. I wanna know exactly what you've been doing."

He shoved her towards the kitchen in the main house and pointed to the designated chair to sit in, so he could loom over her.

"Let go of me…" She wriggled, but his grip was locked in rage.

"Speak up. Drugs and alcohol? You're fifteen."

Severign chose to respond with ambivalence,

which drove her father even madder.

"Don't ignore me. You've been lying. How can I trust you ever again?"

He grilled her mercilessly and quizzed her about how she found the keys. He had never had to scold her this harshly before. Caught between a rock of guilt and a hypocritically hard place. He wrestled with what he could possibly say that would garner paternal respect. Was it too late?

Eventually, Severign built up a well of courage to respond to her lobster-faced father enraged with blood shot eyes.

"I didn't take anything. My friends did. Daisy was here as well, she didn't do anything either. Please don't tell her mum."

"Daisy? Should've known she'd be involved. Her mother? What, that old lush, if I did, she'd forget by the morning. Who else has been here?"

"That boy, Archie, that came over the other day...and his friend, well Mummy's friend's boy, Bertie and a couple of others, I think you met? They're alright." She gulped wishing she had not squealed.

"You mean to say you've had a load of older lads back here for a sesh? It's all there in the bins so don't lie to me."

"They were only smoking."

"You didn't give them my stuff, did you?" said Boyd, blowing his own cover in the process.

At which point he rushed outside to his Den stirring up the kitchen roll under the kitchenette sink for his herb stash. He carefully stuffed it back, satisfied that it was all intact. He took a deep breath and took a slow-paced walk back calmly to Severign.

She gave him an ugly sideways stare.

"You're a lucky young lady, my God. If they'd gotten into my stash..."

"Is that all you care about?"

"Oi. Let's stop shouting. Especially about this stuff. We need to talk. You're fifteen, darling. Do you have any idea how much trouble you're in? I'm gonna have to discuss this with your mother. In fact, where was she when all this was happening?"

"Oh, Daddy please. If I tell you everything, then don't tell Mummy, please. Please."

Severign fessed up to her games, swearing that she didn't get involved, but continued to lie about losing her keys while her mother was out and being too scared to stay in the new house alone.

Boyd paced up and down, rubbing his head, unconvinced. Racking his brain at which action to take to contain the potential fall out, especially where Myrtle was concerned. He was not blameless. He realised for the first time why his brother and family had been so down on him. It was for his own good after all. He was facing his baby Severign displaying similar characteristics to himself. His own family couldn't get through to him. How was he going to manage it with his own daughter?

"So, are you going to tell Mummy? She shouldn't have left me home alone."

"I know, hun. I get it, sneak your friends for a sleepover by all means. But not all this. There's traces of coke everywhere. Do you know what that is?"

"Yes. Mummy's friends do it. I'm not stupid. You both treat me like a child. I know what goes on...and you can't ..."

"For fuck's sake, I expected you to act up some day, but... Are you being bullied? Is that what it is?"

"For the last time, I didn't do any coke'rrr."

"Did you see your mother do coke? You sure about that...or is this another one of your lies?"

"Tch. I suppose you just sat and looked at sunsets in Ibiza then?" she said glibly.

"You are. PUSHING YOUR LUCK, SEVERIGN!" yelled Boyd. "Go to your room. NOW!"

"Sorry."

"I... I've had enough of this. I'm knackered and I need to think. Go on."

Severign crept away, in contorted expression as she passed her father. Almost out of reach from the line of fire.

Then.

"Give me that phone."

Horrified she moaned, "Noooooo..." As she unwillingly slid the phone across the work top.

It was almost game over. She had lost the battle with her father. The war could only be won via her mother. There was no other choice. If only she could ask Daisy or Archie for support. In fact...anyone. Her anxiety quickly shifted to what she would miss out on her WhatsApp group chats. It was unbearable.

*****

Having lived in West London for over two decades, Myrtle had her usual haunts mapped out. Where to go for the best Bloody Mary or red snapper or which local boutiques to hit for less obvious fashion trends.

She had many pockets of friends for various activities, mostly revolving around red wine. With that came a carefully cultivated social life based on post dinner party sit-ups in lovely local homes to exploit a ready-made market – a sitting market.

She sought arrangements with her closet pals, the inner sanctum, to run up £500 debts before she gently nudged collection. As a favour she would offer to reduce the debt if that person would organise a 'party' or 'get together'. An invited Myrtle, turn ups, serves up and hey presto...grams to go. Everybody's happy-ish. This direct selling business model lends itself well to this market.

The midweekers were the best customers, Myrtle learned early on. After come-down-Tuesdays, the come-over-for-dinner Wednesdays invites arranged during the weekend would occur...starters, mains, wine and coke dessert. The routine worked except when she had the theatre run. That was a fixture without wriggle room.

She had been known to turn up to three such evenings, having a starter at one, mains at another before leaving for the dessert run. She would reserve her best clients for this privilege. To stimulate of-floading more grams, she would giveaway heaped lines, loss leaders after which the customer was always right. Right out of it. Meanwhile, the buying decision process skews off kilter, helping to upscale sales.

One such group were the fortysomething women, who had swerved the responsibilities of children. They, unanointed by the stretch marks of childbirth, with time consumed in matters of the 'sisterhood' and gratuity for the blessings of the universe, all in juxtaposition of the self-gratifying pursuit of hedonism...the ones she could count on to be available at a moment's notice. They were identified as her staple clients. Although, they were feast and famine in terms of buying power, they could be in need of an impromptu party pack at the weirdest times of the day or night, like 7am Monday morning, only to reorder by the evening's rush hour. They also had a propensity for detoxing. Abstaining from alcohol, rich food and the doodah, plus a little yoga and well-being thrown in. It made perfect sense to arrange a spa retreat.

Myrtle had managed to sell a watercolour to a customer on the Scottish Borders, so as long as it was anywhere near Peebles, she could make a decent trip out of it. Once the idea had been floated, Myrtle delegated the time-zapping logistics to Helen, a skinny mousey, centre parting, shift dress-wearing advertising editor, who had already built up quite a debt on tick with Myrtle. Always profitable when that fine line between friend and client had been max-imised to full effect. The familiarity of having your mate with supplies on tick took its toll. There can be no doubt, being friends with a dealer had its limita-tions as Helen was to find out when Myrtle offered to shave off some of her debt if she made the spa date happen.

Retiring to Myrtle's room after dinner, the group were relaxed after abstinence, fully detoxified having eaten clean food. They lounged around, proud of themselves, fresh scented, dissolved in their fluffy white robes and slippers all treatmented-up.

"Oh, so needed that. Good call, Myrtle."

"I'll sleep well tonight. That back massage was so good."

"My skin feels lovely after that mud."

"Better than that other mud…hehe."

"Well, girls," offered Myrtle smugly. "Think we deserve a reward for that. I've got two bottles of bubbly down here with our names on. Shall we?"

Despite their best intentions the women could not resist real champagne. The glint of the silver ice bucket and flutes magically produced from below the dressing table was too much to decline. Once Helen egged them on, they had to join in. The first bottle polished off in a matter of minutes. Second bottle laughter brought on a pang for prang. Jayne fessed up to packing some vodka miniatures, ran off and returned to find that she had been saved a Pyrenees heaped line on the side table. The party was on, trying to keep the noise down was unavoidable, especially with Spotify on the go…disco gem Love Don't Go Through No Changes On Me by Sister Sledge hitting the sing-along spot.

"I'm loving Scotland, think I'll come back. Don't know why I've never been before."

"I'm having kippers again for breakfast in the morning. They were lush."

"We missed a trick, we should've come up for that Edinburgh Fringe, heard it's a right laugh."

The women lacked coherence in their chatter, each happy to make mini statements or declarations based on a single word of the last speaker. Just as well as they barely remembered any of it after a session.

At the optimum point of mirth, Myrtle promptly squeezed two nose bags each into the palms of the four gathered before her. Refusing to take no for an answer, she suggested they pay "next time" when they get back to London. It was "all good".

This was a room where the ladies were merry, postponing their sense of bewilderment, blindsided by that additional, unanticipated £140 cost on top of their spa retreat expense.

Myrtle sold the artwork when the client turned

up at the retreat to collect it. All told, a satisfactory couple of days away.

Trotty had refined Myrtle's sales technique to the invisible sleight of hand it had become. Her results were astounding. Helped by her gregarious and charming personality, authentic as it was, the mission was to push those wraps.

*****

A light tap on the door.

"Darling, can I come in?"

Severign sat up on her bed, tucking her laptop away under the pillow quickly.

"Yes, come in," she whimpered, rubbing her eyes hard to make them look sore from crying. Which they were not.

Boyd tiptoed to sit next to her on the bed and holding her head close to his shoulders, gently kissed her forehead.

"My baby girl is growing up," he whispered. "I'm sorry for all the shouting. It's because I care. I'm really worried about the decisions you're making and in some ways I blame myself. I want you to know you can talk to me. Talk to me about anything. I don't care what it is. I'm your friend as well as your dad and I take my job seriously."

Severign was beside herself with relief that her father's maiden speech apology had begun. He had been so mad with her she had expected a roll call of fireworks to go off. She nuzzled in and played victim.

"I'm sorry. I mean it, Daddy. I wanted to talk to you, but since Marisole...well. Also Mummy's been out all the time lately. I can't keep up with her."

"I'll talk to her if you like. I thought you were

happy in the new flat, especially now that waster Marko's out your life."

"I am. I really am."

"Is this Archie, your friend, if you know what I mean?"

"Daddy. That's creepy."

"Whatever he is, is he a good kid? Bring him around again if you like. Let me sus him out for you. I may not approve. But I'll be fair. Promise."

"Daddy, he's so kind to me. He's really clever. He's into his music."

"Easy. One step at a time. When you want to start experimenting, come to me first. I'll have a word with your mother and we'll sort something out."

"Like what?"

"You ain't hurting yourself or starving yourself are you?"

"Please."

"I'm just asking. You hear about these things, Sev. I don't want to miss anything. I'll order something in. Thai?"

"Yes...thanks Daddy. I'm sorry."

"Okay. I'm gonna get up now and give you a shout when it arrives. One more thing sweetie, I think it's for the best if you stay with your mother for a while. I'll meet you for dinner and things, but I think it's for the best for now. Just temporary."

"What? Am I too much of a handful...palming me off with Mummy like this?"

"To be honest? Yes. You've had no stability in a while. It's not forever."

"Daddy, noooooo. I love it here. Mummy's like..."

"Hey. That's the end of it. You need your mother right now."

"No I don't. She'll kick me out after you tell her

everything anyway."

"I'm not going to. I'm going to advise her that you need a woman's presence during your teens. She'll understand. I'll also get her to meet Archie as well. You can stay until your mother gets back, though."

"Why do you want to ruin my life?" snapped Severign, turning away. Gutted, Boyd left the room. He was out of his depth.

*****

Severign waited in the hallway while her father retrieved her phone and handed it back to her.

As she walked towards the car, she could see Myrtle was fuming behind the wheel.

"Get in."

"What do you think I'm doing. Tch."

"Your father has been telling me what you've been up to. A boyfriend? You brought a boyfriend back to your father's? Behind his back? Behind mine? What the hell, Severign?"

"Gross. What else did he say?"

"That he thinks you're smoking. Are you?"

"Nope. I'm not prepared to pollute my lungs by smoking. It's bad enough, the poor city air we're forced to breathe."

"I've not got time for your little games, missy. We'll talk about this at home. And you can give me the phone as well while you're sat there."

The mother and daughter argued the whole drive home, Severign refusing to hand over the phone as a stalling tactic. It was a dangerous journey.

In the flat, the mother's frustration and helplessness began to take its toll on her daughter. She was worn out with it all. It escaped her which punishment she and Boyd had mutually agreed to mete out on her?

Severign wanted the severity of her grounding sentence doled out once and for all. Her plight was languishing in the unknown. Clarity would at least give her something to work with.

But it became apparent for all her mother's dramatic outcries, that there was no mention of the drug taking. How so? The main issue had been mysteriously omitted from the arguments. Was her mother working up to it or had her father had embargoed it.

The focus was on Archie being too old and a bad influence. The perfect distraction to the truth by her father who had bottled it.

She didn't quite grasp why. But who cared? Life was good. Severign could not quite believe her luck.

Her phone was now safely back in her possession…again. Her first call Archie.

"I'm grounded until further notice. Just relieved they didn't take my phone. It's all been worked out. I have to stay with mum for the foreseeable. My Dad got all weird when I mentioned Mummy's habit."

"Tell you what, I don't wanna run into your Dad anytime soon."

"Mummy's been lecturing me about sex, yuck. she thinks she's punishing me by insisting on supervising us. Anyway, as long as we get to spend more time together, that's all that matters."

"Yeah, right."

"When are you going to Spain again?"

"Late September or October when it's cheap. Don't even wanna go to tell you the truth."

It was a bad few days for the pair and their young love. Severign was given short shrift, not allowed to leave her mother's side. They stayed in. They cooked, they baked. She came out with her on short trips, including one to see Liberty, whose assessment of the teenager, much to Myrtle's chagrin, was "she's a beauty, who won't be short of boyfriends"

Back in the Mini, Myrtle could not delay saying the inevitable as they adjusted seat belts.

"Are you? Sorry…does he wear protection?"

"Ugh. Mummy'rrr."

"I just want to be sensible about things. If you're ready for that kind of activity, we need to take responsibility. You're still only 15."

"We?"

"Well yes. If you get pregnant who's going to be left holding the baby - not you I'm guessing."

"Stop there before you offend me any more than you already have. First of all, I'm not with Archie like that yet. We're close. He's in my friendship group… that is all."

"So, what is your father on about then? Didn't you stay with him overnight?"

"Not this again? Like I said. He stayed over to keep me company because I got scared."

"Boyd has more or less left you to me because you're a girl and he feels you need 'woman to woman' nurturing. Such a cop out. I don't want to get the blame for every wrong turn you make. So, we are going to have to do things differently from now on."

"Wrong turn? Like what?"

"I don't know yet. You'd better not be lying."

"I've told you everything. Can you leave me alone now."

"You're still grounded. And four hours phone time."

"I'm going to lose my friends because of you…

you and Daddy."

"You are in so much trouble, young lady. Don't expect any changes when we go to Cornwall. You'll still be grounded."

"Are you gonna tell Granma?"

"Maybe…I haven't decided yet. But if you want to be treated like a grown up, you need to have a good think about your actions. To show you I'm not completely unreasonable, invite your boy round."

"Archie?"

"Whatever his name is. I'd like to meet him. That's an order by the way."

*****

It was love at first sight for Myrtle when Archie turned up with sunflowers and a bottle of wine.

He came across as a bright chap, chatty and enthusiastic and an absolute music geek, which warmed him to her all the more. In comparison to Severign, he seemed to know all the bangers from back in the day.

The conversation flowed quite easily. His own mother would have gawked at the change of personality.

Severign was naturally thrilled at the way her mother and boyfriend were getting on. So much so, Archie had been encouraged to stay and keep Severign company while Myrtle was on delivery runs. This little arrangement was playing nicely into the business. Archie had become a glorified babysitter. Boyd was unaware of this. It was quite the opposite of what he had been banking on.

But as convenient as all this was for Myrtle, she knew she had to insist on meeting Archie's mother.

Dad Is All

After the umpteenth time of asking, Archie could delay it no longer.

The day had finally arrived.

When Archie's mother introduced herself to Myrtle as Evie, they instantly recognised each other. A true blast from the past she was going to deny. There was no way she was leaving her son with this old party animal. Despite this, she could not help feeling a slight relief after all the worrying. She knew Archie was going missing, with no trace of him, or what he was up to or with whom. She had been completely bewildered. Lost.

From their exile to the sitting room, Severign and Archie could faintly hear the awkward conversation.

"I've just come to collect Archie. Sorry if he's been any trouble. I just want to take him home now…"

"Don't be silly. Here. Let's take this into the study."

Myrtle presented Evie with a gigantic glass of Rioja, suggesting they sit down to try and find common ground.

"So where were we…I'm sure I know you?" enquired Myrtle. "Didn't you used to go to Subterranea?"

"NO…" screamed Evie standing up abruptly, her response seeming an overreaction..

"You were seeing Russ Ingram," probed Myrtle. "I'm a friend of Albie's. You know, Albert? Don't you remember? In Camberwell. My God, I know it was bloody eons ago, but you can't have forgotten?"

Evie slammed the glass on the table and yelled after

Archie with everything she had.

The teenagers jumped up from the sofa, worried that things had escalated beyond repair in the other room.

Myrtle shrugged her shoulders at the young couple, as Evie moved towards the door, Archie preparing to follow.

Then the intercom rang, which stopped Evie in her tracks.

Myrtle grabbed the phone. "Oh Libby...I'll buzz you in, but wait downstairs a moment, please..."

But Liberty was concerned enough about the noise she had heard emanating from upstairs, that she climbed the communal stairs and rapped on Myrtle's front door.

Myrtle, terrified of drawing any attention at this new address, especially after the police were called on Marko, quickly ushered Liberty in.

Evie, herself mindful of reinforcements on Myrtle's side, checked herself and quietly said:

"Don't worry, I'm leaving. I'm going."

"Don't I know you?" said Liberty quizzically, "It's Heavenly, isn't it? Heavenly-Angel, wasn't it? How the hell are you? Do you remember me?"

"No!" came the curt response again, as Evie scurried out of the door. "Sorry, I have to go."

"What's going on, Myrtle? Haven't seen her in years, what's she doing here...have you had words? I knew it was her. God, it's been years..."

"That's my mum, you don't know her, her name's Evie, not Heavenly?" said a distraught Archie.

He looked for his knapsack, grabbed it and squeezed Severign's hand goodbye.

"I have to go after her. Never seen her so anxious. Weird. Sorry, Myrtle. I didn't mean to cause any problems."

Liberty, with a deep breath, put her hand to her

mouth. "You're joking, are you? Heavenly's kid?"

Myrtle shook her head at Liberty, in an inference to drop this line of enquiry.

But Liberty, with no concept of the circumstances, blurted out: "Yes, of course. You really resemble your dad. Russ Ingram is your Dad, right? He was, is, one of my favourite DJs of all time. My God? Haha…"

"What?" shrieked a perplexed Archie, instinctively sensing some semblance of a dark truth in what he had heard. Standing right up in Liberty's face, he raged: "Who the fuck are you? You don't know anything about me."

Turning to Myrtle, Archie's eyes pleaded to her to make her friend disappear.

"Mummy…Liberty…stop this," begged Severign.

Myrtle intervened. "Can we all please calm down. Liberty, go in there. Archie step away. This isn't like you. Severign go on, you and Archie sit down."

Myrtle took a breath and composed herself.

"Now listen. This is very delicate. I'm sorry things have turned out like this. But I have to say Liberty is telling the truth."

"Thank you."

"What?"

"I recognised your mother when she arrived as, so it seems, did Libs."

"How could I not?"

"Shush for a moment. The poor boy doesn't know…"

"Poor boy? I'm getting out of here. This is madness… as bad as it is at home. Sorry, Sev. This time I'm really going. Myrtle you're unbelievable."

Archie walked away in disgust.

Myrtle ran after him, pleading. "I thought you would've wanted to know. We're not lying. It's why your mother ran off."

Severign chased after Archie. "Thanks, Mother!"

On hearing the main front door slam, Myrtle wearily summonsed her mate into the study. Sighed as deeper breath as possible and offered Liberty a hastily racked up line. They sat at the desk.

"What the fuck was that all about?"

"Darling, I only wish I knew. Some weird people around. It's Severign I'm more concerned about. Her boyfriend doesn't know who his father is. The poor boy is destroyed, poor lad, and then you turn up and blurt it out."

"I never. Oh dear," said Liberty, giggling nervously. "Shouldn't laugh, though. Fucking hell. So did Heavenly...?"

"Heavenly nothing...I just met her today. She pretended not to know me before you turned up."

"She looks well, though. Slim as ever. So, did I get it wrong, Russ isn't the father?"

"I've no idea. Didn't know she was even pregnant. I have not seen the girl since the nineties...or was it noughties...time flies."

"It flies alright. As I recall there were rumours flying about her having Russ' baby at the time."

"Was there?"

"I can't quite piece the goss together, it was so long ago."

"Never heard a thing."

"She was a strange one. One minute she was everywhere...then she just disappeared off the scene."

"Well, she wasn't the first. We all grow up, don't we. Especially after having a baby."

"You didn't!"

"Hey. I weaned Severign for seven bloody long weeks and the little bust I did have, has perished."

Liberty rolled her eyes then did the line off the desk with a £20 note.

"Have you got anything to drink?"

"Here, have this. Rioja. She barely touched it. Shame to waste it.”

"Bloody hell Myrtle. Is this how you treat your guest on a first-time visit?”

"Thought she was going to toss it in my face at one point. Here...take it with you, and follow me into the kitchen.”

"On a serious note, hun, this place is marvellous. It really is."

"Thank you darling. I still have a load of finishing touches to add. But it's hard to decide how much when you're renting. Can't wait to get our own place."

"You will eventually darling. So, what're you going to do about Severign and her nice young man, then?”

"I don’t know. It's a frightful business for him. I don't want Severign to suffer either as a result.”

"Be careful, they'll blame it all on you for her mistake a zillion years ago.”

"Oh, don't I know it."

*****

Archie and his just shy of 6ft frame lumbered towards his close by Kensal Rise home. He was going at almost three times the pace of Severign who was talking breathlessly behind him...run-walking failing to keep up.

"Babe. Please slow down. Let's talk a second. You're not thinking straight."

"Go home. I have to talk to my mum. Don't follow me."

"I can't let you run off like this, you'll do something stupid. I can tell. Stop a minute."

"No. Go home. I don't want to talk about it with you."

"Archie, please,” pleaded Severign. "I know what you're like. If you go charging in while your mum is still angry, you'll never get the truth."

"I won't get the truth? Obvs. Fuck off."

"Archie, I hate when you swear at me. I know you're mad. Look come back to mine. One more night and then we can make a plan to sort things out with your mother."

"Leave me alone. You don't understand. I need to do this alone. So leave it."

"Babe. Babe. Please stop for a second."

Archie stopped only to spitefully bark in her face.

"It's over, Severign. Go back to your drug dealing mother."

Physically and emotionally exhausted, Severign's eyes glazed over with tears nestling on her lashes. Defeated, she curled her lips inwards. Turned around, she walked away from her first love, heartbroken, sobbing all the way home.

*****

Archie was the first to arrive home, storming through the front door, heading straight for the kitchen. He flung open cupboard after cupboard door, searching for his mother's gin stock. He unscrewed every individual bottle, mostly screw tops, some triple-triple-distilled with corks, and poured the booze down the sink. He wanted his mother to feel as mad as hell too. And sober.

He held back one last full bottle of her oh, so precious gin collection, ready to empty for dramatic effect as she walked in.

"What the hell, Archie?" she screamed as she scanned the kitchen at the empties strewn across the table, work surfaces and floor.

"You fuckin' little shit. What have you done?"

Archie was satisfied that he had got the desired reaction.

Evie stomped her feet and shook her fists, letting out a primal scream of frustration, but couldn't bring herself to look directly at her son, as he sat back, acting the cool customer.

"Stop screaming and shouting," requested Archie calmly.

"I will fucking shout, if I fucking want to…you fucking idiot…what are you trying to do? You know what? You can piss off back to that house. Your little girlfriend's skanky mother can pay for this damage. You ungrateful sod."

"Call me names all you want. Anything but my Dad's name, innit?"

Pacing up and down the medium sized kitchen, Evie was crazed with agony.

"Don't start that shit, I am not in the mood. Is this what all this is about?"

"Are you even my real mum?"

"I'll tell you what, right now, I bloody wish I wasn't. I've done everything for you. I've been Mum and Dad. Better even. You've wanted for nothing. I've done my best. But oh no. Don't you think if your Dad wanted to be here, he would be? He wasn't interested and that's that."

"Stop shouting, sit down."

"Fuck you."

"I swear down, Mum, I'm not going anywhere. I'll stay here until we starve, day and night until you start opening your mouth and TELLING ME THE TRUTH!"

Her sweet baby boy's squeaky voice ebbed into that of a grown man. The deepness in the tone was disconcerting.

She sat on a chair and her chin trembled as she burst into floods of tears.

"Archie. You're killing me. I don't want you to hate me. Can't you accept that sometimes you don't have to know everything. The truth hurts. I live with it every day."

"Likewise. The lies hurt. I have to live with those lies every day. I'm not prepared to do it anymore, Mum. Don't cry. The tears can't help you now. I need answers. I'm a man. A man needs to know his father."

With a heavy heart, clutching her wet face, Evie shook from side to side, undecided. Is this the moment she had dreaded and put off so many times?

The smell of juniper, elderflower and spring flowers wafted in the air. They sat in silence except for the sniffles.

It was quarter of an hour before Evie slowly arose from her chair, kicked a cork across the kitchen floor.

"Wait there."

After some minutes, which felt like a year to the anxious Archie, Evie produced a birth certificate and placed it in front of him.

"Wait a minute. It says here you're Yvonne-Leigh? Not Evie?"

"Yes Evie. Short for Yvonne. My Dad used to call me that."

"Myrtle said you were Heavenly or something? Which is it?"

"It was just a nickname I gave myself. In fact, your father gave it to me. He thought I said Heavenly instead of Yvonne-Leigh."

Archie held the piece of paper, the anticipation on his face as if he was holding a winning lottery ticket. He scanned the certificate intently looking for names.

"So, Starkey Moran is my father?"

"Yes."

She tilted her head up to the ceiling attempting to roll the tears back inside.

'Wow, Heavenly, we finally have the truth."

"Don't call me that."

"There's a DJ called Starkey..."

Before he could finish, she interrupted, grabbed the

piece of paper.

"Yes. He is a DJ. Look, give me this back."

"Hang on a sec..."

"Archie. I cannot do this now. I will tell you the rest another time. Will you let it lie?

Please. For me."

"But I know this DJ. Old school house."

"I mean it, Archie. Don't go digging anymore for now, can we put a line under it for the time being please."

"Okay. Just one thing, though? Why did Myrtle's friend say I look like some DJ called Russ In-somebody?"

"She said what?"

Heavenly was jolted by the revelation. Quick to shut him down, she asked: "Russ? Give me a break. How could they remember anything, off their faces the whole time? Snouts always in a nose bag, them two. Tch."

"Is that why you didn't want me to go into music? In case I ran into my Dad?"

"No. No. That wasn't it."

She tapped on the delicately printed document, the ramifications of which could have profound consequences on their relationship forever.

"Come on. Let me take this. You go and get washed. You stink. I'll bring you up some hot choc and we will talk about this again soon. Promise. I'm very tired."

"I'm an adult. I don't want a hot choc. You and gran have been lying to me all this time. All the times I've had to listen to the whispering behind my back. You would just look at me and fob me off. I knew you were hiding something. That was the worst. I feel betrayed by my own family. I needed to know the truth. It's all I ever wanted."

"I'm so sorry son. I love you, you know."

"Sometimes I wondered whether I was adopted. I was just wishing you'd fess up. All this time it's been hanging over me. You just don't get it."

"I'm sorry. I am so sorry."

With that she folded the certificate, tucked it into her shorts pocket as she set about mopping up, wishing this moment was washed over as well.

"I'm sorry. I am. I'm so sorry."

"Look at you, all you're bothered about is clearing up. Well you can't clean this mess up just like that. It's my life you've been fucking about with."

"I know. I'm sorry. Sorry, I didn't know what to do back then. I promise I'll talk another time. Let's just go slow."

"Slow? Fuck's sake, I've waited almost 18 years."

Archie banged his fist in defiance on the granite, hurting himself in the process.

"You know now and that's all that matters. We will deal with the next step together. Live with it a while first. It's a lot to take in."

Heavenly spoke quietly, determined to de-escalate matters.

"Go on, take yourself off to your room. Speak in the morning before I go to work."

Archie was desperate to Google his father, but wanted to do it on a brand new day after a good sleep. He chanted "Starkey Moran" under his breath, not so much in a smug air of achievement, but for the first time in a sense of self.

Mother's Midweeker

The blackout blinds in Archie's bedroom twinkled under the flashing LED lights from all his gadgets. Red or green, amber or clear ones. This was a new morning, like no other in his life.

Starkey Moran. He stared at the ceiling cuddling the name of his father in his mind.

A DJ and producer he had heard about. Someone he thought he could look up to. Respect even.

Archie sprang out of bed and scurried to search his father's name on his mobile. At once he was bombarded with Starkey Moran's social media profiles. Interviews upon interviews, track listings, past gigs, forthcoming gigs and blogs and so many images. All the brands that he was associated with.

He raced through the hyperlinks. No sooner had he opened one page than he would open another, barely reading the info, before he clicked out and into another again. The images became his main focus. He tried to see beyond the screen and connect. Enacting how they would be, face to face for the first time. He could tell that he was already taller than the images of man looking back. Their hair was different, Starkey's build slight in comparison. He tried to make similarities subjectively. When he had exhausted this search. He included the year 1999 and carried on. Older pictures came up. He hoped to see pictures of Starkey with his mother but they failed to show up.

He could hear his ex-clubber mother's footsteps on the landing. His view of her had altered significantly, in complete contrast to the adulation he felt for his father. He recognised that his mother's drinking was rapidly getting worse since working for the gin company. Was he a product of one of her drunken sessions or was she a bit of a caner, like Myrtle back then? He was more than certain that she was not taking anything, it was just the demon drink that blighted their lives. He mentally documented all the alcohol ladled phases of his young life by bottle… the red wine evenings, the Prosecco times and now the gin, in that order.

He jerked at the light tapping at his bedroom door, made more irritable by his mother's attempt at light heartedness referring to him by his birth name. "Arch? Arch-Angel baby?"

"Leave it…Heavenly," he responded sarcastically, wincing at the oh so imaginative biblical references. The pieces were fitting together.

She took the dig nobly. She accepted there would be unsavoury reactions, as he came to terms with events. "Just wanted to say, if you want to talk, we can do it after work this evening?"

"Can you leave us alone please."

"Alright, then, was just checking in. Shall I bring you up a Diet Coke?"

"No, thank you."

"Well, if you change your mind about that chat…we can go to Nandos or something later if you like?" replied Heavenly. She was wasting her time.

*****

Armed and overwhelmed with his new identity, Archie washed his old self away in the shower. He was Starkey Moran's son. Pride that welled up in him like a bespoke tailored jacket fitted perfectly.

He couldn't wait to tell Severign…he was going to have to make good after the way he had behaved, but he knew he could make it up to her. Everything was possible.

He was right. Severign had texted him all through the night and sobbed after every message sent. The relief to hear from him was more important than the content. He was sorry and that was all that mattered.

They agreed to meet at the park. To talk. Archie needed a sounding board.

"He's a DJ. My Dad is a flippin' DJ, can you believe it? Hahaha. After all that."

"I've never heard of him I don't think so, anyway. But I'm so glad for you, babe."

"I feel…I feel different. You know, like, I can't explain it. I'm just so excited that he's into music. That's gotta be where I get it from?"

"True. The talent must run in the family."

"Not if my Mum had anything to do with it. You know she called herself Heavenly, says because my Dad called her it, when she was young. Then she named me Arch-Angel. I mean what the actual fuck was going on in her head? It's nuts."

"Arch-Angel? Not Archie? How beautiful. I love."

"I'm sure I told you that before. My mum's a weirdo. It's official."

"Erm, you've not got the only dibs on that front. So what're you gonna do now?"

"Not sure yet. Look him up. Contact him, somehow. Find his agent or something? I won't stop until I find him. She's brought this on herself."

"Why don't we ask Mummy? She's bound to know somebody who knows somebody. She's probably his friend on Facebook. Shall I ask her for you or are you keeping this low-key for a bit?"

"Oh yeah, your mum's going to know something. I was thinking of Bertie asking his old man. They probably still play the same gigs. I'm excited about this Sev. I can't help it."

"I can't help thinking this isn't much fun for your mum, Archie. Your new father might have lot to say. It could be tricky, babe. Needs more thinking time than you're giving it."

"Whose side are you on Sev?" exclaimed Archie.

"I'm trying to help, babe. It's a lot to take on. I think it's been kept a secret for a reason...sorry, just want you to be careful."

"You sound old."

"Thanks."

"Can I come back to yours? Will your mum let me stay? Is she mad at me?"

"Yes, please come back. I think she's feeling guilty. Not sure if she's in tonight. Let's get your things and if you're already there she can't say anything."

"We can ask her about my dad then..."

"Sure..."

*****

"Dinner? Sounds good, is it alright if I skip the starter, I've got Severign."

"You're welcome to bring her. She's too big for the other kids, but if you don't mind?"

"She's almost 16 going 60, darling. Last thing she wants is to be around toddlers. I'll sort her out first and come over later. Is 8.30 too late?"

"That's fine. It's just our usual mother's midweeker, ha."

"Great. What are the numbers?"

"About five of us, counting you."

"Hahaha, love a school night supper. What's on the menu?"

"It's pretty informal, hun. Red mullet and a Cajun salad. Trying out a new recipe. It's wasted on them to be honest, they eat naaaaaaathing, dahling."

"Hahaha…don't fret, I'll get my nosh on as they say. Do they say? Hahaha."

"Bye darling. See you later."

*****

Myrtle could smell burning toast from the outside hallway, before she even put the key in the door.

"Severign, Severign…darling, are you burning toast?"

She was met by a wide-eyed daughter, presenting a cremated, sun dried tomato toastie to her boyfriend.

"Oh, hi Mummy. You're back!" She reached to hug and kiss. This was new.

"Hello Myrtle. Sorry I ran off yesterday."

"That's okay darling. Is everything alright now, between you and your mother?"

"Erm, sort of."

"One minute…" She headed towards the kitchen, then shouted, "Severign put the extractor fan on, how many times? What a bloody mess…"

"Sorry, Mummy, Archie was hungry."

"I'm going to make some dinner, is Archie stopping?"

"Is that alright, Mummy?"

"Come here a minute. Stop the yelling."

Severign diligently obeyed, adopting favour mode.
"What're you making, then?"

"Thought veggie sausage and onion gravy?"

"Sounds yum. Can he stay a few days? Please?"

"Well I'm not so sure what his mother will say. I'll have to have a chat with her. It might be too soon. He's welcome to stay for dinner, though."

Just as Severign was gearing up to negotiate further, Archie popped his head round with an empty side plate.

"Finished. Shall I put this in the dish washer?"

"Thank you. I'm making veggie sausage and onions, save your appetite."

"Lovely."

It took Myrtle a couple of clumsy nudges for her daughter to take the hint and leave her to a friendly chat with Archie.

"Can you fetch a chopping knife from the thingy, there?"

She pointed to the knife holder.

"Here you go," said Archie, on the charm offensive. "You know, I think you're a really good cook, Myrtle."

"Severign says you want to stay?"

"If that's okay? I hate it at home."

"If it was down to me you could move in permanently, darling. But Boyd would have something to say about that. As for Heavenly, she'll never allow it."

Watching Myrtle's nimble artistry chopping onions on the board, he considered what he could possibly say to persuade her otherwise. He replayed his dramatic exit, chasing after his mum. How could he make it all better?

"Were you on the rave scene same time as my mum then?"

"Yes, but possibly for a lot longer than she was. She's a beautiful lady."

"Can I tell you something. I did find out who my father is. You might know him?"

"What? Last night? Oh my God."

"D'ya know him, he's a DJ. I've already told Sev."

"Are you sure you want to tell me. You don't have to."

Myrtle wiped an onion-fuelled tear using the back of her palm.

"It's Starkey Moran. You must have heard of him?"

"Yes. I have."

"Have you met him? Do you already know him? That other fella you mentioned, she denied having anything to do with him. That's when she told me."

"I don't know what to say. How do you feel about that?"

"I'm pretty excited about it. I'm dying to meet him. He doesn't even know I exist."

"Why all the secrecy though? Your mum must have a reason."

"That's what Sev said. I want to contact him, but don't know how to go about it. Was thinking Bertie's Dad might know."

"Eli will for sure. I could ask him for you. Tell you what, leave it with me. I'll ask around. This is a very delicate situation so if I were you, I wouldn't try contacting him via social media."

"I need to talk to him soon. I can't hold it in now that I know."

"Yes, but you don't want to ruin things by going about it the wrong way."

"Thanks, Myrtle. I really appreciate this."

"Don't thank me yet. I shouldn't be getting involved. So, here's the proviso. Nothing happens until we've had a chat with your mother."

"Proviso?"

"It means there are conditions to my helping you out, dear."

Severign peered around the door.

"What are you two talking about still?"

"Shoo, shoo! Get out of my kitchen both of you."

"Thanks Myrtle," said Archie, with a cheeky wink.

*****

"My God, is that the time? Kids, I've got to dash. Please clear up properly after you've eaten. Have you seen my leather jacket, darling?"

"Which leather, the biker or the other one?" asked Severign.

"Found it."

Myrtle mad-dashed, grabbing her earrings, portfolio case and other bits together, sliding on a pair of white cowboy ankle boots and a designer cuff. An expensive present from an ex-boyfriend.

"Right. Behave yourselves. Don't wind your father up."

"Don't worry, I won't pick up, I'll text him."

"Don't tell him Archie's here. No offence, Archie. Don't stay up late. I'll be back by eleven. WhatsApp me if you need anything. In case of emergency call Auntie Libby. And Archie, do call your mother. Okay, then. That's me done. I'm off. Kisses...mwah."

Myrtle scarpered down the stairs to the front door, car keys jangling as she left the building.

*****

Every two or three weeks, Tuesday or Wednesdays, a few mums in Queens Park organised play dates with a difference. Each mum took it in turns to have all the kids for a sleepover, while the others gathered in one and another's houses. Whosever's husband wasn't around, mostly. As usual, the wine always flowed and two by two they would sneak into a downstairs loo for a 'livener', the best course of the night.

Like the 'fortysomethings', dessert always on offer, barely eaten. Business or not, this was one evening Myrtle was happy to be a part of. She missed those days when her daughter was a toddler."

Above the babble and chatter, Myrtle's ears pricked up when she heard a line-up of DJ names mentioned for another trendy, boutique festival.

"Sorry, Di. I must just ask Charlotte something."

"Charlotte darling, do you know Starkey Moran?"

"Yes, I do. He's great, isn't he? A friend of yours?"

"No. Not directly anyway. Do you mind if I pull you away for a minute?"

Under the influence, Myrtle charmed her way around Charlotte to obtain the DJ's number. It wasn't difficult. His details were in her contacts now and was going to make one young man very happy, which meant bonus points with her hard-to-please daughter.

Myrtle teased the ladies with a few complimentary snorts, then a handful of orders predictably followed.

Having almost sold another painting, with an enquiry to buy, this was turning into a bountiful evening overall. But after two hours she packed up her things and left…home by half ten.

Hearing the ascending footsteps. Archie and Severign rushed about the kitchen, desperate to tidy up.

"Mummy, you're back early?"

"Shall I make you a coffee?" offered Archie.

"Thank you darling, but no. There's a half a bottle somewhere in the fridge. Bring us a glass."

Myrtle, the worse for wear, but grade 6 rather than 10, steadied herself on the counter. Severign rolled her eyes in embarrassment.

"I'll get it Archie."

"Called your mother yet? Does she know you're here, darling?"

"I texted but she hasn't responded. She's probably asleep," lied Archie with ease.

"Hmmm? Well, keep trying."

Then a dramatic pause…

"So, young man…I have Starkey's number for you, but you didn't get it from me."

Archie jumped and hollered…punching the air.

"Steady on, boy. I'll give it to you in the morning. I don't trust you not to do something stupid tonight…sleep in the guest room. Severign check the bedding for me, and no sneaking about. Nightie night," she chirped, stumbling out, boots off, wine glass in hand.

Remixed

He strode to the beat, staring at Google Maps, hoping to look cool in his best pair of checkered Vans trainers and a Superga hoodie...determined not to be late.

Arch-Angel was on his way to meet Starkey Moran at Nobel Studios in Barnes.

Charged up by a momentous surge of happiness, when Starkey's blue tick confirmation receipt of his message had responded immediately. He still couldn't believe the ease of the WhatsApp conversation, and looked back at it again to make sure it was real.

[Hey Starkey, u don't no me. I'm Heavenly's son. I wondered if I could meet with u for a chat. Arch-Angel.]
[Erm, Yeah, sure. How is Heavenly? Is she alright?]
[Yes she's ok. But I wud like to talk to U pls.]
[Of course. I'm in London for a few days, but working flat out. Could you get to Barnes?]
[I will find it. Wens gud?]
[Anytime next couple days only. Daytime. I will send link to the studios. Text me before you come over.]
[Thnx. Means a lot.]
[Great name btw.]

As excited as Archie was at meeting his father, he was also pumped to be hanging out at a pro studio.

The euphoria of the connect was palpable. With

those few words Starkey seemed pleasant and trusting. It warmed Archie's heart. He became instantly attached.

Archie played out how he imagined the meeting of his life would pan out. A father and son remixing tracks, producing floorfillers... perhaps playing a gig or two together.

When Archie was buzzed in, his heart almost burst through his mouth. He realised he had not taken a breath. He followed the directions and a short, silver haired figure in a long, grey low neck t-shirt appeared ready to shake hands. His ruddy sailor complexion bordering on lobster, a backdrop to his bright piercing blue eyes, was the first thing Archie noticed.

The greeting was the briefest of hugs that usually followed a 'man-shake'. An anti-climax to the tear-jerking film moment Archie dreamed about. He half expected Starkey to guess what he had come to say. It was weird.

The studio, a windowless chamber, devoid of nature, as if one potted plant would devalue the sonic creativity process. Ideal conditions for testosterone tech engineers to breed and multiply from jam sessions to dancefloor to studio to online.

They sat opposite each other like strangers, Archie on the couch, Starkey on a drummer stool, sipping a couple of cans from the nearby mini fridge.

"So Arch-Angel is it?"

"My mum's idea of a joke. Everyone calls me Archie, actually.

"Don't knock it. It's a great name. How is Heavenly?"

"She's alright, when she's not pissed."

"Whoa, fallen out with her, have you?"

"Her name's really Evie. She said you called her Heavenly."

Starkey cleared his throat, stalling to think what would be an appropriate answer.

"Your mother and I used to work together. I'll admit I did give her the pet name Heavenly- Angel. See, she kept the biblical theme on."

"What were you to my mother?"

"Wait a minute. I don't really know who you are. Are you even who you say you are? Show us a picture of your mum. Do you have one?"

"Yes. I'll show you," tutted Archie, picking out a selfie she sent a month or two back. "That's her."

Seeing Heavenly beaming away, her dark hair off her face, catapulted Starkey to those heady days at the Bells On Agency. He was a successful multi-award winning music producer these days, but this grounded him back to a time of his blonde ambition.

"She's still a beauty, hope you don't mind me saying."

Archie rolled his tongue in his mouth. He was here to talk about their bond and not Starkey's romantic stroll down memory lane.

"She never talks about you. Sorry."

"Okay let's cut to it. I only agreed to see you because I was worried about Heavenly. I don't understand why you're here."

"I'm here..." Archie braced himself. "I'm here because Mum says you're my father?"

Starkey coolly adjusted his jeans, screwed his mouth up, then replied.

"Hold on, hold on a second, mate. How old are you? You must be 17...18, right?"

"Soon. Eighteen, yes."

"Keep going. Explain to me slowly what's gone on

here. This is madness. Sorry no offence. First off, do you not know who your father is? Who brought you up?"

"Mum brought me up on her own, and sometimes with my gran in Northants. She came to London when I was about six. That's all I've got. She never tells me anything. I've asked her a million times to tell me who my dad is. Then, the other day, things got on top and she blurted out your name."

The blood drained from Starkey's face. To hide his shock, he dived in the fridge for two more beers.

"Archie. Your mother should be having this conversation with you. But as you're here now and I think it's for your own good, I'll tell you what I know."

"Please. I'm tired of the secrecy. You don't know what my life's been like. I've only ever wanted to get to know you."

"Well, I gotta say…you seem like the kind of lad, I wished I had had. Correction… wished I could have."

"What do…you…"

"This is going to hurt a bit. I'm not your father. Sorry Archie. Sorry to be so blunt, it would take a miracle."

"Are you denying it. Should we get a test or some-thing?"

"Hang on, hang on. Listen. Don't interrupt me. I just want to get this out and hopefully send you on your way to find the truth. Every boy deserves to know who his real father is."

"I don't like the sound of…"

"Wait. I had a girlfriend, a fiancé who…long story short…had a car accident because of me and wasn't able to conceive children after that. You can imagine how it broke her and her family's heart. Anyway, it's very complicated but 'Rora, sorry my girlfriend, we had a very toxic relationship after that. You got a girlfriend?"

Archie nodded.

"It's hard work isn't it? Anyway. I was racked with guilt and thought, that I would have a vasectomy to even things up. You know, the snip? It always bothered her that I would leave and have kids and an idyllic family life with someone else. It haunted me and haunted her. I didn't tell her, just went ahead and had it done one afternoon. When she found out, instead of feeling better about everything, things went the other way, well...long story...I did say. Look. The upshot is, when I was seeing your mother, I was already sterilised. I can't have kids. You are not my son, Archie. Sorry."

Gone Rogue

Nestled in an Über on her way back from an evening of gossip with Jo E, Heavenly Angel was feeling more herself than she had for years. She even contemplated giving up alcohol and eating more.

Now Archie had seen his birth certificate she felt lighter. She could forgive him for crashing at Myrtle's place, convincing herself he was blinded by love, certain to return when Severign broke his heart. It was time for a fresh start with her son. She was determined to win back his trust.

She was ecstatic to see the light on in the kitchen as she opened the front door. Her beautiful boy was home.

"Arch-Angel, baby boy, you're home?"

Archie barely grunted. A mother knows when her baby cries no matter how old. Heavenly ran over to look at him sat at the kitchen table, head down, slumped like a test dummy, post-crash.

"Oh my God, are you alright, darling? Have you taken something?"

He shrugged her away from him as she tried to examine his face. His eyes were red, sore and puffy. A look she recognised. This wasn't weed, this was heartache.

"Darling, darling..."

She kneeled down uncomfortably in her leather skinnies to look up at him.

"What's upset you, hun? Is it your girlfriend? Savanna, is it?"

"No. And her name is Severign. Can you at least remember that?"

"Hey, hey, hey," she cajoled, trying to appease him. "I don't want to fight."

"I'm going to ask you one more time, Mum. Or is it Heavenly-Angel? Yvonne-Leigh? Or shall we stick to good old Evie?"

Heavenly Angel bowed her head and stared at the floor.

"Whatever it is, whoever you are?" continued Archie. "I want you to tell me…once and for all…tell me who my real dad is. No more lies. You're killing me, Mum. I need to know and you're the only one that can."

Archie sniffled, trying to hold back more tears.

Heavenly moved across the kitchen, strained by her son's state of mind. She assumed he knew enough to keep him onside, but her answer could mean losing him. If she told him the truth, she could lose him forever. In silence she made herself an elderflower gin and poured Archie a glass of water.

Then she began solemnly.

"The other night you found out your father is Starkey Moran, right? I can tell you, that I had an on/off relationship with him. I loved him so much, but, if I'm honest, it was irrational. He was too was into his work. He was and is a successful DJ. He was obsessed with music, which was what I liked about him at first. But to him, everything else came second. I have no idea what he is like now, but I'm afraid he was a selfish bloke. Emotionally immature. I thought he cared about me, but when I realised he was using me…I…I hated him. It's a strong word, but I hated him. I felt just as you do now. I am sorry. I am so sorry. I should have told you. The biggest mistake of my life."

Archie's green eyes welled up again.

"Mum, why?" said Archie quietly. "Why can't you tell me the truth just one time. Starkey isn't my dad. You're a liar and I hate you. I'm going to live with Severign and you'll never see me again."

Heavenly look terrified.

"I'm not lying Archie. Listen to me. What makes you think what I've said is a lie? I've told you everything. Ask Jo E. She knows all about it. I swear I'm telling you the truth."

Archie got to his feet. It was an empty threat to leave. This was his home. But the uncertainty about who he was or where he belonged plagued his outlook. Starkey was not his dad. He was back to square one. Now his own mother spinning a web of deceit at his expense was impossible to bear.

He attempted to go upstairs to his room, muttering under his breath, "I've met him. He told me himself."

"Come back here. What was that?"

"I SAID I SAW HIM TODAY! HE SAID HE IS NOT MY DAD!"

The rage was back.

His stunned mother stood paralysed in shock.

Part of her longed to see him again, but the craving disappeared in a single heartbeat.

The dejected young man carried himself to his room. An exasperated mother crept behind. She sat outside his door, scrambling for words.

"What...what did he say to you?"

She was certain he had headphones on and couldn't hear a word. She asked again.

"What did he say?"

When she didn't get a reply, she talked to him through the door. It was like a run through of what to say. She was listening to her own breath, rehearsing what to say before she heard it out loud.

"I do everything for you my precious one. I remember how I cried when I had you. I loved you so much. I didn't even know...anyway. Hope you can hear me because I need you to hold onto this part. I always loved you."

She stalled, her phone was buzzing. She ran down to answer it. Jumping each step, for a millisecond hoping it was Starkey. Then worry turned to her mum's health. She saw that it was only Jo E and picked up relieved.

"Jo E?"

"I'm outside, hun"

"What's up?" Heavenly, opened the door as her pal barged in.

"I'm okay. It's you I'm worried about. Is he...?" Jo E looked towards the ceiling pertaining to Archie.

"Yes, he's in his room. I'm alright, though. I can't believe you've come over?"

"I couldn't leave it love. Last time you were like this, all the mixed messages, we found out you were pregnant...what's wrong this time?"

"I've told him everything. I've told you everything. I can't cope."

"Let's sit down on the sofa...I can't take those hard seats. Babe, something's not right. I can't put my finger on it. That's why I'm here. I think you should call him down. Talk to him in front of me."

"Noooooo. I can't do that. It's all too sensitive. He's been to see him..."

"See who?"

"Starkey. It's fucked him up." Heavenly rubbed her ears.

"Fuck me. I knew it. I could just tell. So, what happened?"

"I don't know. He wouldn't admit he was the father. He hasn't changed."

"You need to talk this through. Do it now. I've been through similar remember. The lies create more problems. Don't allow any time to pass, while he's a teenager. Yvonne, you've got to get this right. Call him down."

"Jo E, I know you mean well, but I'll handle it from here. Thanks."

"Bet you don't. That boy has been lied to all his life. We're doing this. You'll thank me. Call him. I'm here for both of you. I'll call in sick."

Sometimes Jo E was worse than her mother once she got the bit between her teeth.

"A fucking pain is what you are. I'll go and get him, but if he doesn't answer..."

"Shall I go up? He'll answer to me."

"I'm so scared, Jo. Really, really scared I'm going to lose him. I couldn't bear it."

"Shhh...leave it to me. You trust me. He trusts me. I love him like he's my own, you know that. I won't hurt him. But it's time for an intervention. He needs to know."

No music, no headphones, lying on his bed almost in state, a numbness had befallen Archie, only the LED lights dancing about him.

The doorknob twisted back and forth and a scratching on the door alerted him out of his stupor.

"Arch, Arch love...?"

What the hell was Auntie Jo E doing there.

He rose and gave his favourite pretend Auntie a

limp hug. She wiped his face and demanded he made her a herbal tea like he used to.

Heavenly dared not look up from the sofa. Her future was in the hands of her best friend. The closest person to the history.

"Do you want one?" asked Jo E.

Heavenly nodded quietly.

"Bring it over to me, Arch. I want you to talk to me and your mum."

He stood facing them. Refusing to sit down, but agreeing to talk.

The talk was heavy and drawn out. Archie communicated from an emotional place. No one interrupted. After one hour no closer to resolving the issues Jo E applied some objectivity just to speed things up.

"Why did you believe Starkey? You still haven't told us."

Realising his error, the teenager spluttered out Starkey's vasectomy tale. Before he could divulge the full story, he watched his mother run over to vomit in the kitchen sink. She whimpered like a lonesome puppy.

They were unified in their efforts to assist her. Even Archie showed some empathy at that point. It suddenly dawned on him that she didn't know.

Returning to the sofas, this time all three sat down, Jo E sipping on a glass of water. In a frail voice, Heavenly, gingerly asked Archie to explain again.

"I can't remember what his girlfriend was called, but she couldn't have kids, that's why he did it. That's all I've got. But, aside from anything else mum, I'm still no closer to finding my real father. My birth certificate is void. I'm invalid."

"Okay, Arch, I promise you, no way did your mum

know that."

"I believe you, Auntie. But you ask her who my dad is? I can't ask anymore.'

Jo E pursed lip and raised eyebrows had reached a dead end. Looking over at Heavenly, she mouthed:

"So...what now?"

"A DNA?" demanded Archie.

"No need," replied Heavenly, calmly. "His name is Russ Ingram. He doesn't know. I never even..." Unable to finish the sentence, she broke down and sobbed.

"Alright...it's alright," consoled Jo E. "We should get you guys some family counselling. They'll help you through the next phase. Archie, you'll get some answers with professionals and they'll advise you how to deal with things. Now that you've heard all this. See it as a new beginning. Give your mother a break. You can see it's tough for her too."

Archie professed he was "tired" and "over it" and took himself off to bed, concluding that Starkey and his mother were "a couple of pathetic idiots".

His whole world was a hoax, orchestrated by the cruel deception of his own mother - gatekeeper of the source of his DNA. For what selfish reason did she make this judgement call and assume it was for the best? All about protecting herself. His feelings clearly did not come into it. A lonely place to exist. If Archie cut himself loose from her ties it would be like floating in space away from the mothership. It scared him to think of it. He did not feel he had the courage to inflict this on himself. The only alternative was to continue to exist on Planet Betrayal.

Abandoned.

The sapling of acceptance took root in the young man. He was done with it. His future will be devoted to music and Severign...the only loves that mattered.

*****

"Jo, he hates me. He's gone."

"He needs you. Let him be. Have patience. He'll be back. You've got to watch your drinking, though."

"I don't get it? Why did Starkey give me that money when he knew I wasn't pregnant for him?"

"Oh God...that was bad. He never had any intention of going with you to the clinic, did he? D'ya think he just wanted rid of Russ' baby?"

As the cruel possibility dawned on Heavenly, the front door slammed back against the wall. The ghost of a summer past.

Acknowledgements

Kerry Coburn for all your hard work and support.
Mom & Dad (RIP), Prudence, Winsome, Carole, Glasford, Blair (the apple of my eye...and...wow! Blair...well done!) Josh and Colleen.
My English teachers, Mr Duxbury and Mr Krayer.
Disco, jazz-funk, boogie and house music.
The Masons Arms, The Whippet Inn, North London Tavern, The Salusbury, The Paradise, The Parlour, The Cow, The Westbourne, London, The Cock & Bottle, The Chamberlayne, E&O, The Electric, Pizza East.
Mr Brandon Block – for the book that inspired so many others.
Matt for the editing...and also his patience and encouragement in the development of my writing.
Aine Doris for spurring me on...mwaw!
Thank you:- Lisa O'Meara, Lilamani De Silva, Jane Adams, Ann Smith, Dr Sara Sylvester, Jenny Small, Scorpiane Gayle, Lea Mason, Raquel.
iPhone X.
Reena Qureshi.
Oprah Winfrey and Vanessa Feltz.
Brenda Emmanus.
The Notting Hill Carnival.
Gilles Peterson.
Paul Trouble Anderson.
Tony Blackburn.
Bulldog and the Birmingham jazz-funk crew.

George Michael.
Aretha Franklin...Respect.
RIP Keith Flint.

Thanks to the hospitality of the following
venues, where I sit, sip and write:

Adriana's W10
Portobello House W10
Cafe Porto W11
St Marks Park W10
The Eagle W10
The Mall Tavern W11
The Earl of Lonsdale W11
Leon, Nottinghill
Timo (Portobello)

About The Author

Jaqi Loye-Brown has lived a storied life.

From signed-singer to indie record label A&R...BBC researcher to supporting artist in Bridget Jones' Diary...and youth worker to DJ/club-owner (ex) WAG, Jaqi travelled professionally and personally through many of the most defining moments of the nineties and noughties.

All these experiences and more make it into her novellas...a unique remix of chick- lit with edge and homage to the first era of rave.

A compelling new voice in British fiction, Jaqi's narratives are suffused with humour, sex, extraordinary happenings and maverick characters as infuriating as they are endearing. There's also more than a hint of nostalgia for a time that will mean a great deal to readers of a certain age, and a certain musical persuasion.

An accomplished poet and spoken word artist, Jaqi has published three novellas in her Portobello Novella Series and is now developing a number of projects set to shine a new light on contemporary issues.

Also on MT Ink

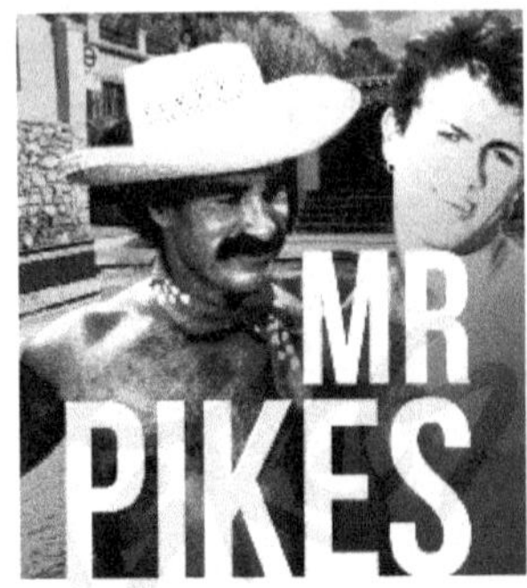

Mr Pikes - The Story Behind The Ibiza Legend - Tony Pike

The playboy who built himself a playground reveals all in his electric memoir.

The iconic hotelier reflects on a life of hedonism and the globe-trotting back-story that influenced his creation of pioneering Balearic boho bolthole, Pikes.

Pike talks candidly about his relationships with hotel guests and friends including George Michael, Freddie Mercury, Julio Iglesias and lover Grace Jones…and also goes exclusively behind the scenes at the Club Tropicana video shoot.

The Life & Lines of Brandon Block

Brandon strips back his dramatic life as we chart the meteoric rise of a cocky schoolboy from Wembley who became an Ibiza legend along the way. A symbol for an acid house generation of excess, Brandon headlined a clubland era that changed the lives of millions.

His spiralling drug habit peaked at an amazing ounce of cocaine a day but somehow he survived to tell the tale. Includes extra chapters published in 2017 as Brandon prepared to enter the Celebrity Big Brother house.

One More: A Definitive History of UK Clubbing - 1988 - 2008 - Matt Trollope

The story behind the superclubbing generation features the era's resident DJs including Jeremy Healy, Sasha, Judge Jules, Danny Rampling, Graeme Park, Brandon Block and many more.

With promoters behind clubs like Venus, Renaissance, Hacienda, Golden and Miss Moneypenny's they answer the question: If tonight was your last ever gig, what would be your 'One More' track?

DJ Whore - Jaqi Loye-Brown (Portobello Novella Series 1)

In pre-Millennial London Heavenly Angel, the alter-ego of disillusioned Yvonne-Leigh, worships at the altar and ego of DJ Starkey Moran.

Jaqi Loye-Brown's debut DJ Whore is set in the late 1990s, peering over the shoulders of the movers and shakers, fakers and takers. Through her Portobello Novella series, Jaqi explores the frayed hem of a cutting edge era, tiptoeing through a clubscene rarely explored in a chick-lit.

DJ Wags: Housewives of House - Jaqi Loye-Brown (Portobello Novella Series 2)

Some yummy mummies are not like the others. What lurks behind the domestic bliss of middle-aged party parents? Piper Blair and Dande Lyon's friendship comes to a head when their loyalties, love and lifestyle are tested under the spot-light of reality TV.Middle-aged, middle class and functioning...just! From Kensal Rise, Queens Park and Westbourne Grove to Ibiza and back again. From disco to discord all the way

Road To Recovery - Terry Dunnage

Terry Dunnage had been scooped up...and dumped in Hell. His favourite uncle flicked at a cigarette lighter, trying to ignite more petrol. The fire felt like a bomb had gone off. A huge swirling backdraft engulfing both of them, Uncle Vince defiantly resisting Terry's desperate attempts to drag them from the suffocating flames.

An inspirational comeback from deep depths of life-threatening burns, trauma, dispair, family tragedy, legal battles, financial ruin and depression.

At mt-ink.co.uk or all Amazon sites